Dirty EMPIRE

Empire Nightclub #3

K.A.TUCKER

Editing by Hot Tree Editing

Cover design by Shanoff Designs

Published by K.A. Tucker

DIRTY EMPIRE

From internationally bestselling author K.A. Tucker comes the dark and sexy Empire Nightclub series

Mercy Wheeler and Gabriel Easton's sordid tale continues in Dirty Empire as Mercy finds her loyalties tested and Gabriel's attempt to break free of his family's legacy comes with unexpected consequences.

Dirty Empire is the third book in the Empire Nightclub series and should be read after Sweet Mercy and Gabriel Fallen.

ONE
MERCY

I WANT *to be better for you. I want to deserve you.*

Gabriel said those words to me. He whispered them as he pressed his forehead against mine, and my heart fluttered at the thought that this reprehensible man I've somehow grown fond of could—would—change his criminal ways for *me*. In my mind, he was making me a promise. The kind you make when you're in love with another person and want to change.

And then the private jet we were about to climb into exploded into a fireball and the reality of who Gabriel is and the kind of life he leads came crashing down.

Now, sitting on Gabriel's couch hours after being surrounded by a circus of sirens, emergency workers, and city and state law enforcement, I can hear the blast of metal, feel the intense heat of the fireball, and smell the ash and black smoke as if I'm still at the airfield. But it's Gabriel's and Caleb's pained screams for their perished friends that fill center stage in my numbed mind.

"Mercy."

It takes me a moment to focus on Gabriel's handsome

face. He's perched on the edge of the coffee table in front of me, his calloused hands woven through mine, a somber expression pulling his brow tight as he studies me. I recall the first time I encountered those stormy blue eyes at Fulcort Penitentiary. We were there to visit our fathers: mine, a kind, loving man wrongly convicted of murder; his, a hardened crime boss who should be serving twenty times the sentence handed down to him. Whatever Vlad Easton was sentenced to is a misdemeanor compared to what he's done in his lifetime.

I remember thinking Gabriel a wildly attractive man, with that chiseled jaw and plump lips and playboy swagger. But he was affiliated with a dangerous inmate and therefore someone I wanted to stay far away from. His indecent proposal a week later—that I stay with him in exchange for his providing protection for my father—only confirmed it.

And yet here I am.

"Are you all right?" Gabriel asks, his raspy voice unusually soft.

I nod absently, though the last thing I feel right now is all right.

"She needs something to take the edge off." Gabriel's brother, Caleb, hands him a tumbler glass of amber liquid. Gabriel wordlessly slips it into my grasp. It must be the scotch Caleb cracked as soon as we strolled through the front door. I only noticed because it's not his usual thirty-eight-thousand-dollar vodka. I thought it strange at the time that he bypassed his favorite. Funny, the things you notice when you're in shock.

I'd rather drink gasoline than scotch, but I tip my head back and pour it down my throat anyway, relishing the burn of hard liquor, barely aware of the taste.

"That a girl," Gabriel croons, smoothing a hand over my bare knee.

"Ready for another?" Caleb tops his own glass.

I swallow and shake my head. Only then do I notice my best friend is missing. "Where did Michelle go?" There's a hint of panic in my voice. Did she change her mind and take off?

"I sent her up to my room to take a nice, hot shower," Caleb says, his tone dispassionate.

Normally I'd have some quip, some warning, some ring of an alarm inside my head at the idea of Michelle getting too close and comfortable with Gabriel's brother, a manwhore by anyone's standards. Now, all I can think about is how Michelle could have already boarded that plane with Caleb while she waited for me to arrive.

My best friend could have died tonight, simply for being connected to me.

We *all* could have died, if not for road construction that made Gabriel and me fifteen minutes late. Pylons and fresh asphalt literally saved our lives.

And in the aftermath of the explosion, while we sat on that tarmac as emergency vehicles raced up to deal with the fiery carnage, and we ducked away from view of countless news cameras that congregated outside the gates to capture the scintillating story, Michelle remained startlingly calm. She told the police who questioned us nothing beyond the surface truth—that she was joining her best friend for a weekend in Vegas to celebrate my having written my last college exam. She didn't so much as hint at the other, more vital details that she is *fully* aware of—that she was traveling with a well-known crime family and that every minute of the trip had likely been bought and paid for with drug money. She played clueless, beautiful arm candy to perfection.

When Gabriel instructed our driver to bring us home, Michelle didn't demand to be dropped off at her house, she didn't tell me to get the hell away from her. She clasped my hand and said she was going wherever I was going, even as her fingers shook.

I'll never find a friend like her again.

And tonight, I almost lost her.

But Gabriel and Caleb... they *did* lose people.

"I'm sorry about Felix and Finn," I offer, my voice sounding hollow to me. I didn't know either of them well, and can't say that I liked what I knew of them, but it was clear by Gabriel's and Caleb's horrified expressions after the explosion and their somber demeanor since that the twins were important to them. "And about your crew, too." The pilot and a flight attendant also died in the explosion. Four people, in total. All of them simply because they were connected to the Easton family. All collateral damage.

I'm connected to the Easton family.

How long before I become collateral damage too?

My stomach roils at the thought. "Who tried to kill us?"

"It was a fuel leak," Caleb says without missing a beat, dumping his glassful of scotch down his throat.

"That was *not* a fuel leak," I counter evenly. Does he take me for an idiot?

Gabriel's mouth twists. "No one's trying to—"

"Don't feed me the same bullshit you tried to feed the cops. They didn't buy it either." I saw the looks, the whispers of "Easton" on lips. Everyone there knew who Gabriel and Caleb are. It's virtually a guarantee that their investigation will conclude that plane was rigged with a bomb. Unless, of course, Gabriel buys a more palatable report for insurance purposes and to avoid unwanted attention. I wouldn't put it past him—there doesn't seem to be *anything* they can't afford—but with the FBI rolling up in their black sedans, I doubt there's a price tag affixed to sweeping this one under the rug.

Gabriel's eyes flash to Caleb, where a warning glare awaits him. In the past few weeks, Gabriel has slowly begun disclosing details about his sordid life that I'm probably better off not knowing. He's hinted enough for me to know his family didn't come by their money honestly, that while the club he and Caleb own might be a legitimate a business, there's likely plenty running out of it that isn't. Hell, I've watched *Ozark*. They're probably laundering drug money through there.

But I won't get much out of Gabriel about tonight's attack while Caleb is here to toss out lies and guard his little brother's tongue.

"Why don't you go and take a shower? I'll join you soon." Gabriel squeezes my thigh.

Normally the promise of his expert hands on my body sends my hormones into overdrive. But I'm not ready to be dismissed so easily yet, not when my life is at stake here, too. "Do you have *any* ideas who did it?"

"Like Caleb said, it was an accident."

My anger flares. "What's wrong? Are there just too many people who want you both dead to keep track?" I imagine the list could be long.

"Come on." Gabriel stands and tugs my hands until I'm on my feet too.

"I don't feel like a shower—"

"For fuck's sake, would you listen for once?" His soft-spoken words from only moments ago have evaporated with impatience.

"Sure. After you stop lying to me!" We had an agreement that Gabriel wouldn't peddle false tales about his life and who he is. Mind you, we agreed to abide by a "don't ask, don't tell" rule. I guess I'm the first to break the agreement, because I'm asking.

A metal click sounds, pulling my attention to the bar. My body tenses at the sight of Caleb checking a handgun bullet chamber, his handsome face a mask of grim determination.

I'm sure there are plenty tucked away all over this mansion, at the ready just in case. While it's not the first gun I've seen—the handgun Dad made me buy for home protection when he went to prison is still wrapped in a shoebox and stuffed into the back of my cramped apartment closet—it's the first time I've seen either of these two brandishing them so openly. That's odd, now that I think about it, given who they are.

"My brother and I need to discuss a few things, and you can't be a part of that conversation. Why don't you go and take that shower. *Now.*" Caleb's voice is eerily calm.

Neither Easton man has ever given me any indication that they would physically hurt me if I didn't comply with their demands, but things are different. Dangerous. Maybe giving these guys attitude isn't the smartest move at the moment.

Gabriel's looming height and muscular frame suddenly make me feel small and powerless. "Come on. I'll be right behind you," he whispers. He leans in to press a kiss against my temple before coaxing me toward his private wing of the house with a firm hand pressed against the small of my back.

I steal another glance as Caleb pulls a second gun from somewhere below the counter. *I'll be right behind you, my ass*. My gut tells me these two will be conspiring over possible suspects and how to exact retribution—the kind that doesn't involve law enforcement and arrests—late into the night. I'm not sure how I feel about that, given their targets nearly killed me tonight.

I don't know how I feel about *anything* anymore.

Including Gabriel.

My legs are wobbly as I head for the bedroom, hoping a hot shower will help me shake this icy feeling that has seized my limbs.

TWO
GABRIEL

I WATCH MERCY'S SLIM, sexy frame disappear around the corner. With it goes all semblance of composure. "Who *the fuck* tried to kill us tonight?" I force out between gritted teeth. My fist grips Mercy's empty glass as I fight the overwhelming urge to launch it across the room and watch it shatter into a thousand shards. Adrenaline has been coursing through my veins double time for hours, ever since someone blew up our plane—and our two best friends, along with two innocent staff members.

Finn and Felix are gone. My gut spasms at the thought. It hasn't sunk in yet. I still half-expect to wake up Sunday morning to those two idiots strolling through our front door, looking for liquor to drink and women to screw. That's not going to happen though. Instead, their sweet mother is going to be receiving the most expensive floral arrangement we can buy ahead of us showing up on her porch with a blank check to pay for a double funeral.

There will be plenty of time to mourn them. Right now, we need to figure out who put a hit out on us and when they're going to strike again once they learn they've failed.

"Take your pick." The muscle in Caleb's jaw tenses. He's simmering in that dark mood of his, the volatile one that is unpredictable, chilling, and can be downright deadly if provoked. I was relieved when Mercy finally left. He wouldn't lay a hand on her, but his words can be just as destructive, and she's already been through enough tonight. "We know the cartel didn't do this. Those fuckers would rather send our heads to Fulcort in a care package for Dad. So it's Uncle Peter or it's the Perris. Simple."

Our father's brother, who's been maneuvering to take over the entire Easton empire, or our family's sworn enemies.

"You *really* think Uncle Peter would blow up our plane like that?" Our own flesh and blood?

"After we dropped that picture of him in bed with the Feds into Dad's lap?" Caleb snorts. "We basically signed his death warrant. He probably sees it as tit for tat, and he's got nothing to lose, especially if he's guilty. Plus, we all know he likes to blow shit up."

And now that Dad's behind bars, if Uncle Peter takes us out, he and our rat cousins will control Harriet, Dad's code name for the lucrative family drug business. He definitely has motive for eliminating us from the equation, aside from old-fashioned retaliation—something he's always been fond of. "But has he even figured out we're onto him? Dad would have warned us if he'd put a hit out on Peter, wouldn't he?"

It's been almost a week since my last visit to Fulcort, when I informed Vladimir Easton that his own brother sold him out to the FBI in a power and money grab. It went over as well as to be expected. Dad turned heads with his barking and then stormed out, and we haven't heard from him since. Has he put feelers out to see if it's true and Peter betrayed him? Has he demanded Peter explain himself? Or has he decided the crumpled picture speaks for itself and dialed up his favorite reliable henchman, Bane, the one man he trusts to do his dirtiest work?

"That hateful old fuck wouldn't take too long to make his move. But, no, I can't see him putting Bane into play without warning us. You know, since we're his pride and joy and all that," Caleb mutters, his loathing for our father oozing through each syllable.

"So then how could he be behind tonight?"

"Maybe Peter caught wind of our arrangement with the Perris. We knew things were going to move fast once we set those wheels in motion." Caleb's gaze is locked on the night sky beyond the wall of glass in our living room. The view from atop Camelback Mountain of the Phoenix city lights below is the reason we bought this mansion in the first place. That and the privacy we're afforded all the way up here, to live however we want without prying eyes.

But now there are unseen enemies somewhere outside; watching, waiting for the next opportunity to take us out. Tonight was a close call. The closest we've ever had.

Caleb is right. The night we hatched the plan with Merrick and Vince Perri that would finally free us from our family businesses and a potential future behind bars, we knew there would be family members—including our own—who would retaliate if they caught wind.

But is that the case? If it is, how the hell would Peter have found out and so fast? Who talked? "Something doesn't add up."

Caleb tips his head back to polish off another tumblerful of Scotch. He reaches for the bottle.

"I need your brain working tonight."

He scowls but stalls short of pouring himself another drink, reaching instead for the pack of cigarettes. He lights up. It's a sign that he's rattled. He *never* lights up in the house. He doesn't even like it when others smoke around him. "Maybe Peter had nothing to do with this then. It's time we give our new friends a call and ask them a few pointed questions about explosives."

"I don't see the Perris for this." At least, not Merrick or Vince. Those two are like us. They want to get *out* of the family business, not in deeper. They're the one who came to us with answers about our mother's death that we've wanted for almost two decades: Camillo pulled the trigger on the gun, but it was their older brother Miles who brutally raped her beforehand.

"Camillo wouldn't think twice," Caleb croaks through an exhale. A coil of smoke sails from his lips. "If he or that psycho son of his found out about our little chat with Merrick and Vince, if they knew our end game? They'd make a move now to get rid of us once and for all."

Miles Perri, the oldest of Camillo's four sons, is indeed a murdering psychopath. Jury's still out on Leo.

"If Miles found out about our arrangement, he'll kill his brothers."

"That's why we need to touch base, stat." We haven't reached out to Merrick or Vince to tell them we won't be arriving in Vegas tonight. We wanted to wrap our heads around the situation first before we stepped out waving a "you missed us, you cocksuckers" flag in case it *is* the Perris behind this. For all we know, their oldest brother has them tied to chairs as he extracts information.

Caleb's phone chimes with a text. He promptly checks it.

"Farley?"

"Yup. All clear."

I sigh with relief. Empire is closed on Wednesdays,

which made it easier for our security team to haul in the dogs to confirm that whoever tried to kill us tonight didn't also wire the three-story warehouse. It's one thing to blow up a small plane with a handful of people in it. It's pure madness to light up a packed nightclub. But we aren't sure yet who we're dealing with and it could very well be a madman. "We need to keep security detail on both the club and our home until we get figure it out. Is he on his way here?"

Caleb nods through another long drag. "Three guys will stay on this place, and three will come with us."

I have a feeling it's going to be a long night. "Who do we call first—Merrick and Vince or Dad?" Despite what we may think about our patriarch, he's done a few laps around the someone's-trying-to-kill-me block. He'll have solid advice.

Caleb scowls at me. "Dealing with Dad is not a fucking phone call, Gabe. This is an in-person conversation. A private one."

I groan. "Yeah. Okay." *Fuck.* Caleb and our father in a room together in the best circumstances is a terrible idea, which is why Caleb never visits him. My head's already hurting, thinking about witnessing this rare encounter. "I'll call Donny. He can make it happen." We've lined the Fulcort guard's pockets with enough cash over the years to earn us the occasional private meet outside of visiting hours. I feel sorry for the poor schmuck though. Vlad won't take kindly to being dragged out of his cell bed in the middle of the night. He's likely to sit up swinging. "Say we'll be there in two?"

"Three. Maybe four, if we have to shake a fed tail." Caleb flicks his half-burnt cigarette into an empty tumbler.

"We need to have a friendly little conversation with Uncle Peter and Vic first."

"Like, *go* there to see him?" It's my turn to stare at Caleb like he's the idiot. "If he's behind this, he'll be waiting for us."

"I hope so." He reaches below the counter and pulls out two more gun clips.

"Just a friendly conversation, huh?" I can't help but chuckle, though none of this is funny. With the mood Caleb's in, he's liable to shoot our cousin between the eyes without so much as a hello. And the sharp set of his jaw makes me think that's exactly what he's planning on doing. Those two have never gotten along, and Vic is a cockroach. The world could do without him.

But I can't help wonder how much worse will things get before sunrise.

Will we both even be around to see the sunrise?

"Farley and the guys will be here in ten and then we roll." Caleb nods toward my side of the house. "You want to give her a heads-up that we're leaving?"

"If I want to wake up with my balls attached, yeah." That woman has a sharp temper, and the Easton name doesn't seem to strike fear into her. I admire that about her.

Caleb eyes his wing of the house, where that cute blond is showering, and I already know where his head's going. Both heads.

Normally I'd warn him to keep his dick in his pants. Mercy has been adamant that my brother not add her best friend to his infinite parade of mindless lays. But after what happened tonight, everyone's on edge. I'm not about to cock-block him, not when he's this wound up. Maybe blowing his load in someone will clear his head enough to not start a war tonight.

Besides, Michelle has been eye-fucking him since the night they met. She practically dry-humped his lap the night he drove her home, if his version of events is accurate. That my brother didn't take advantage of that is a damn miracle.

"We hit the road in twenty," he announces with grim determination, marching for his wing.

I grin. "Thought you said ten."

"Your dick can thank me later."

Twenty minutes. Just enough time to make sure Mercy remembers me in case I don't come back.

I WASN'T sure what I'd be heading into when I stepped to my bedroom—Mercy, packing? Aiming to launch the alarm clock at my head in a fit of rage? The anger is strong in this one—so I'm relieved to hear the steady stream of water from the bathroom.

I settle at the threshold to the sprawling shower stall and admire her naked body, my hands itching to grip her tiny waist where it flares out into round hips. Those curves might be my favorite on her. Those or the dip in her back, just above her tailbone. Every time I drag my tongue down her spine and reach that spot, she tenses with anticipation.

Then again, those long, toned legs of hers are also a favorite of mine, especially when they're curled around my body.

As are her tits, filling my palms.

And that tight, inviting pussy.

Who the fuck am I kidding? Every square inch of this woman's body makes my mind go blank. Especially when she's in the shower.

She peers over her shoulder to catch me admiring her. "I thought you'd already be gone by now." She says it coolly, as if talking about a household errand I need to run. But I catch the slight hitch in her voice at the end.

"Just waiting for security detail to show up. You and Michelle will be safe here tonight while we take care of this."

Awareness flashes in her chocolate brown eyes. There's no point lying to her; she's figured out we're on someone's hit list. But the less she knows, the better, even if being kept in the dark pisses her off. A lot of what I do pisses her off.

She turns back to face the tile wall, her fingers weaving through her strands of long raven hair. "So much for trying to change."

I can't believe she's throwing my words from earlier tonight back in my face. "This is different."

"Is it?"

"Yeah, it is." My irritation flares. Can't she see the truth? "What the fuck do you expect us to do? *Nothing?* Wait until they try a second time?"

Silence answers me.

"Maybe you don't care if I'm dead, now that you've got an account full of money to pay for your father's lawyer. Is that it?" Have I misread Mercy up until now? The way her body molds again mine at night, her soft smiles when she wakes and sees me next to her, the way her lips linger on mine every chance she gets. I thought something was happening between us, but maybe I'm wrong about everything and she still hates my guts.

My stomach churns with that thought.

She spears me with a scalding glare. Her pretty, full lips pry open, and I brace myself for one of her tongue-lashings, but she pauses. After a moment, she shakes her head.

I finally see fear in her eyes. I've been waiting for it to arrive all night. All I want to do now is scoop her up into my arms and make her believe it's all going to be okay, that I'm not going to let anyone hurt her.

Has she been stewing over all the directions tonight could have gone, like I have? Not that it didn't already end in tragedy, but I've had an endless loop of horror-show scenarios playing in my head: Caleb and Michelle, happily sucking back drinks on the plane while they wait for us to arrive; Michelle, tucked into her seat, ready to surprise Mercy when she boarded.

Mercy, boarding the plane ahead of me.

Every time that last possibility so much as glances across my mind, I'm hit with the urge to lean over and empty my stomach. It's quickly followed by the need to interrogate Uncle Peter with a gun barrel pressed against his forehead.

If we're right about this, I'll pull the trigger myself.

Regardless, whoever set us up to die tonight will pay the price.

I take a deep breath to calm myself. The last thing I want to be doing with her right now is fighting. "You know how to use a gun?"

She nods. "My dad taught me before he went away."

No doubt because of the shithole apartment he let her move into. The entire place should be torched. Maybe I'll have to take care of that once I've taken care of my current mess. Or at least have it condemned. She'll be forced to stay with me for good.

I think I like the idea of that.

But what's beginning to matter more to me is that Mercy likes the idea of that, too.

No, not just likes it.

Loves it. Loves it enough to not decide she's had enough, that she wants to leave. Could I fault her? No. But I also don't know if I can bring myself to let her go.

Fuck, Caleb was right. This woman has her claws in my heart.

I'm not losing her.

"I'll be back in a few hours. I'm leaving a Glock on the nightstand for you. We'll have guys stationed around the perimeter and the house locked down. No one's getting in here. It's just a precaution, but you won't need it." I add after a moment, "Just don't shoot any of my guys. Too many people have died already because of us tonight." My throat clogs up with thoughts of Finn and Felix.

Gone, just like that.

Will there even be anything to put in their caskets?

Whatever anger and fear radiated off Mercy evaporates as her face fills with sympathy. She leaves the warm spray of water to close the distance. Drops of water hang from her thick fringe of eyelashes as she gazes up at me. "Did you know them long?" she asks in a whisper, reaching up to toy with strands of my hair.

"Since we were kids," I answer gruffly. I'm surprised by the way my eyes suddenly burn with emotion. I have to look away—down, over Mercy's naked body, over her hardened nipples and the gooseflesh springing across her wet skin—so she doesn't see. Christ, those two were some of our oldest and most trusted friends, but I didn't really appreciate how much they meant to me until now. I definitely can't remember the last time I felt like shedding a tear over *anyone*.

After my mother died, maybe.

There's no place for men who cry in the Easton family, my father had drilled into our heads over the years.

"You know, it's okay to show how much you cared about them," Mercy croons softly, coming close enough to press her forehead against my lips while keeping space between her slick body and my clothes, as if trying to keep me from getting wet.

"I'd rather show you how much I care about *you*," I hear myself say.

She pulls back, and her eyes flash with surprise.

I don't have time to console Mercy—or myself—the way I want, meshed in my bedsheets for the next seven hours. I seize her tiny waist, pulling her flush against me as my lips fall on hers. The kiss turns frantic almost immediately, our tongues and teeth slipping and sliding and clashing and smashing in a graceless tangle. My greedy hands squeeze her curves, the moisture that clings to her flesh soaking through my dress shirt.

But it's not just me who suddenly can't get close enough. Mercy's fingernails scrape at my chest. She fists the oxford cloth, popping several buttons as she stumbles backward toward the stream of hot water, yanking me with her.

I kick off my shoes as I let her lead me in. A shower, however quick, will feel refreshing after hours of sitting in dry desert heat. "Caleb will be banging on the door in fifteen minutes," I warn. Knowing my brother, he's already balls deep in her friend and racing for the finish line, making the most of being alive for the moment.

"He'll have to wait," Mercy murmurs against my lips, fumbling with the rest of my buttons until they're unfastened.

We should be doing this in Vegas, in the penthouse suite of the Mage—the hotel and casino that Caleb and I are looking at purchasing. It's another step in our bid to move away from our family's drug business and into full legit territory. That's where we were heading tonight, ahead of our meeting with the Perri family tomorrow.

She peels my shirt off my shoulders, breaking our kiss long enough for her heated gaze to drift over my chest. She doesn't have to tell me; I hear her sigh before her lips are back on mine and her deft fingers are tearing away at my belt buckle and zipper as if she can't get me undressed fast enough. Tugging my pants and briefs off my hips, she drops to her knees to pull them down my thighs. I brace myself with my palms against the tile and chuckle as she curses with irritation and yanks at the wet material.

My laughter chokes off with the first swipe of her tongue across my tip.

"Fuck," I groan, letting my head fall back and my eyes shutter for a moment. There isn't a woman in existence I'd rather have sucking my cock, and I've had plenty to compare against. They all blend together, for the most part. But Mercy's mouth? Just the thought of her on her knees in front of me would be enough to make me come.

I peer down to find Mercy's eyes locked on mine as she sets to work on me, strands of wet hair plastered across her gorgeous face. As much as I love this woman's lips around me, the only thing that might help calm this brewing storm of emotion is to bury myself deep inside her.

Guiding her mouth away with a hand cupped beneath her chin, I seize her slight body and lift her up... up... off the shower tile floor. She grips my biceps with her hands and clenches my hips with her thighs as I pin her against the wall. I don't waste another moment with foreplay, plunging deep into her, earning me a gasp and soft moan.

"I don't want you to leave tonight," she whispers, her lips pressed against my ear, her arms wound around my neck as our bodies gyrate hard against each other. There's a hint of desperation in her voice.

"Trust me, I'd stay right here all night if I could." *Right here, in your wet heat.* I cradle the back of her head with one hand to dull the rhythmic bump against the hard tile, pleasure radiating as I thrust into her over and over again.

Mercy's cries reverberate through the mammoth shower stall, growing louder as I fight the urge to unload into her, desperate for her to come first.

Her body tenses within my arms with the sound of a fist pounding against my bedroom door. "No. Not yet," she growls.

My impending release rushes through my groin and along my spine, an uncontrollable force that spurns my hips harder and faster. I reach down between us to slide the pad of my thumb across her clit, intent on coaxing an orgasm out of her.

She slaps my hand out of the way, her jaw set with defiance.

I chuckle. "Sorry. But unless you want an audience...." I didn't lock the door, and Caleb's been known to kick back and watch before.

"Goddammit." She bows her head and watches me plunge into her. It only takes a few moments before her inner muscles are squeezing my cock in a pulsating wave and I'm bursting inside her with a deep, guttural groan.

Her lips are lazy as they drag across my cheek in an aimless kiss. "Please don't go," she whispers. "I have a bad feeling about this."

My stomach clenches at the pleading in her voice. "I don't have a choice. We have to deal with this tonight, before anyone has a chance to make another move and something worse happens."

"You'll come back though, right?" Her body is relaxed within my arms, and yet her legs still grip me tightly, as if unwilling to let go. "You won't let anyone hurt you?"

"I'll be fine," I say, hoping fate doesn't prove me a liar. "I'm more worried about someone hurting you." Her wet hair has molded to half her face. I push it off her cheek, tracing a sharp cheekbone with my fingertip. "I'll *never* give *anyone* that chance again. I swear to you, as long as I'm breathing, no one will *ever* hurt you. If anyone tries...." I let my voice drift, my threatening words unspoken. There's no need; I think it's pretty clear.

I'll kill them with my bare hands if I have to.

Mercy hesitates, words on her lips but not escaping as her gaze searches my face.

"All right boys and girls. Hate to break this fuckfest up," comes Caleb's booming voice.

I expect to feel Mercy tense against me and shriek—rightfully so—but she doesn't afford him so much as a glance, her eyes curious and unreadable as she studies me.

I steal a glance over my shoulder to find him standing at doorway into the bathroom, dressed in fresh clothes—all black, like a criminal with a plan—his arms folded across his chest.

He gives me a pointed look, unfazed by the fact that I'm bare-assed and buried full-hilt inside a woman. "We've got a long night ahead of us, Gabe. We've got to jet."

"Two minutes." I turn back to settle my lips in the crook of Mercy's neck, inhaling the floral scent of her body deeply, hoping it sticks with me until I see her again. "He gone yet?"

"Yes." She sighs. "Does he go out of his way to be a pervert?"

I chuckle. "It comes naturally."

Mercy doesn't match my laughter though. She seizes my jaw within her palms and levels me with an aching look. "Promise you'll be smart tonight, Gabriel." Her lips are red and swollen and glistening, and a big part of me wants to ignore my brother, the late hour, and our pressing schedule and let her wrap those around my cock after all.

"I'll be smart. I promise."

I wish I could say the same for my brother.

She worries her lip, and I have to wonder if she's thinking the same thing. That thought doesn't linger though before it's replaced by a soft smile.

I wasn't wrong.

Mercy doesn't hate my guts at all.

THREE
MERCY

"This view is next level." Michelle grips the tumbler of scotch with two shaky hands as she peers over the rail at the view of Phoenix below us, the ice cubes Caleb dropped in before handing it to her tinkling against the glass. I always wondered what might unnerve her. Apparently, her plane exploding moments before she embarks, courtesy of a mob hit, is the ticket. It might have taken a few hours to settle in, but my normally feisty friend is nowhere to be seen, replaced by this subdued, somber interloper.

"It is." I peer through the wall of windows into the house, where Farley, the enormous security guy with the tattoo on his trunk of a neck, is stationed. He made both Easton men look like gangly prepubescent boys when he strolled in, his shoulders filling the width of the doorway. The guy hasn't stopped scowling since he stepped through the front door. I'm beginning to think that's his permanent face. God knows where Gabriel and Caleb found him. Hopefully not prison.

He's the only one in the house, but two slightly smaller versions of him—minus the neck tattoo—are out there in the dark, watching over us. Possibly watching *us*, standing here in matching white terry cloth robes, the effort to dig out clothes from our luggage a seemingly exhausting task.

These guys are here to keep us safe, I remind myself. And we need to be kept safe because we're associated with the Easton crime family.

Will that ever become commonplace for me?

"Did Gabriel tell you where they were going tonight?" Michelle asks after a moment.

I shake my head.

She hesitates, as if she knows better than to prod. Or maybe she's not sure she wants an answer. "Did he tell you *anything*? Like, about who might have done this?"

He didn't have to. They left in the SUV, armed and trailed by another SUV with three guys who didn't bother to introduce themselves or even acknowledge us. They weren't going out for a casual drink at the bar. "No, and it's better that way, trust me." Somewhere between Gabriel suggesting that I don't care if he dies and letting me drag him into the shower, I decided I don't want details of what he and Caleb are planning as retribution for the plane and the death of their friends. I just want the threat gone, and I want Gabriel to come back to me in one breathing piece.

And there was a time when I wanted to murder Gabriel myself.

Who the hell am I becoming?

Michelle nods but says nothing else, occupying her lips with small sips of the drink Caleb poured for her before he left. She's even less of a scotch drinker than I am, but nothing about tonight makes any sense. Especially not the tender kiss Caleb pressed against her forehead and the way he stroked his fingers through her wet blond hair in the moments before they left, armed with loaded guns. It looked like he was capable of affection.

"What happened between you two?"

The glow of lights around the pool afford me a glimmer of Michelle's small smile.

My apprehension swells. "It's not a good idea. You don't *know* him." Flash after flash of Caleb's shocking behavior—greeting me in the kitchen buck naked, screwing that woman on the patio chair while his friends watched—flood me. I'm sure those examples are relatively tame in the world of his sexual proclivities. Michelle may be wild, but she's playing in Little League. Meanwhile, Caleb has gone pro.

She smirks. "I got to know *one* part of him pretty well, however briefly."

Crap. I can't stifle my cringe fast enough. "I hope you made him use a condom—"

"Yes, *Mom.*"

"I'm serious! I just don't want to see you get hurt."

She looks pointedly at me. "I almost blew up tonight. Next to that, screwing Caleb doesn't seem all that dangerous."

I squeeze my stomach tight to try and quell the nausea that stirs. "I wish you'd never got pulled into this." I've already made a mess of Michelle's life by introducing her to them. If something happens to her, I'll never forgive myself. "Fine. As long as you know Caleb isn't going to give you what you want. He's not a frog waiting to be turned into a prince, remember? Giant, warty toad." Possibly with syphilis. "He doesn't do relationships." I hesitate before I add, "I promise you, he'll be screwing another woman within the next twenty-four hours."

She flinches at my words, and I momentarily regret saying them. "Relax, it was just the one time. It's not a big deal. It's not like I'm going to fall in love with the guy. I'm not an idiot."

Her words deliver an unexpected punch to my stomach. Is that what's happening to me? I care about Gabriel, that much has become glaringly obvious. When he suggested that I don't care if he survived, that I'd be happy to take his money and run, I realized I hadn't given the money sitting in an untraceable account to pay Justin DeHavilland's legal fees a second's thought. All I've been dwelling on since I stepped under the stream of hot water was the thought of Gabriel *not* in my life anymore—not waking next to him, not feeling his skilled hands on me, not hearing my phone chirp with his annoying texts all day long that aren't annoying at all.

Worse, my stomach has been in knots since Gabriel kissed me goodbye and strolled out the door. It hasn't subsided, and I'm sure it won't until he strolls back in unharmed.

I think I might actually be falling in love with this scoundrel.

"What are you going to do?" Michelle asks, as if reading my thoughts.

"I don't know." It was one thing to agree to this twisted arrangement when it was a simple matter of meaningless sex and comfort in exchange for my father's protection. But it has become complicated—far too complicated. There are real feelings involved. And now I have to worry about mob-style hits?

If I were smart, I wouldn't be standing out here, admiring the view. I'd be shoving every last belonging into my suitcase and preparing to hightail it out of here. The sooner I'm away from Gabriel, the safer I'll be.

Even as I consider this, there's a voice in my mind—or

maybe it's a feeling in my gut—that knows I'm not going anywhere, and it has nothing to do with Farley guarding the door.

I steal another glance into the house, to where the man watches us intently. A shiver runs down my spine. Protection or not, he reminds me too much of some of the inmates locked up in Fulcort.

Michelle's right. A woman would have to be an idiot to fall in love with either of the Easton men. They're criminals. They're out there right now, hunting down *other* criminals.

I know this, and yet now that I know them, I see them less as that and more as just people in my life.

Michelle winces through her last gulp. "God, I don't care how expensive this is, it tastes like ass. At least it'll knock us out."

I hum with agreement, though I already know I'm unlikely to catch a wink of sleep, alcohol-induced or otherwise. Not until I know Gabriel's okay.

FOUR
GABRIEL

Uncle Peter has lived in a sprawling brick house in Biltmore since the mid-1990s. We used to hang out here all the time, back when our mothers would sip fruity cocktails by the pool and we didn't want to choke our cousins on the daily. Back when our father and Peter were brothers grilling Wagyus and puffing on Cohibas together, not trying to bury each other.

The house beyond the front gate is pitch-black as I ease the Lincoln up to the curb. Not a porch light, not a glimmer deep within. Nothing but the glow of the solar panel lanterns leading up the lengthy driveway. "You think they're waiting for us in there?" I keep our vehicle in Drive, half expecting a hailstorm of bullets to pepper us at any moment.

"I would be," Caleb murmurs, but then frowns, first at the house, then at the security camera trained on the street, then on the Aleppo pines and Arizona ash trees scattered over the three acres. Aunt Rita used to go on and on about how she wanted a forested feel to Mom, who'd smile and nod, and then comment privately that Aunt Rita had an unhealthy obsession with wanting a forest in the middle of a desert. Mom was too kind to call the woman out for what she is—a goddamn fool. "Something's off."

"Your head, on account of all the alcohol you inhaled," I mutter, annoyed.

"Shut the fuck up. I mean it." He scowls, jabbing the air with a long, manicured index finger—a secret of my brother's that I like to hold over him: he goes to the spa weekly for a good ol' mani pedi. "The Mercedes is parked out front. They never leave their cars outside, especially not at night."

And especially not with a seven-car garage to fill. "You're right." Years ago, during heightened tension with the Perris—after Uncle Peter detonated their restaurant with dear old Nonna inside making gnocchi—someone wired his Jaguar to go boom. The unfortunate sucker he hired on for additional security measures was the one who discovered it—of course, he didn't live long enough to realize that.

Uncle Peter spat on the ground and declared the Perris cowards for tiptoeing in under the cover of night to set a bomb.

Pot. Kettle.

I study the house as Caleb did. "You think he wired the whole place to blow if we showed up?"

"You kidding?" Caleb snorts. "Peter'd have to listen to Rita bitch at him for the rest of his miserable life. He'd rather lance his eardrum."

And that woman's lips never stop flapping.

Caleb drums his fingers along the doorframe in thought. Behind us, Farley's crew waits in their SUV for our instructions. They're all ex-military. They've faced every kind of enemy-territory situation we can only imagine. They'll scale that wall in seconds if we order them to.

And they could end up dying for it.

Enough people have died because of us tonight, and my brother's right—something doesn't feel right.

I check my watch. "We can make it to Laney's before the doors shut if we leave now." The strip club Vic uses to clean money is in a seedy area half an hour away, and it's almost a guarantee that our cousin is there, drunk and demanding one of the girls suck his stubby little dick. Getting Vic to admit they rigged our plane will happen a hell of a lot sooner than getting Uncle Peter to confess.

Caleb picks up on my train of thought quickly. "Let's roll." He opens his window and gestures to the guys to follow us.

"HAVEN'T SEEN him at all today. Last night, either." The skinny bastard behind a desk three times too big for this office throws his hands up, his devious eyes darting between us and Moe, the smallest of Farley's guys and probably the most lethal. "I swear!"

Caleb and I share a glance. Vic pays the strip club manager to lie for him, so we have to assume he's lying now. But we also didn't see our cousin when we made our way back here, and there aren't a lot of places to hide in this dive. A couple private rooms, a shady corner or two, and the girls' changing room.

"You mind if we take a look for ourselves?" Caleb says lightly. *Translation: keep your bouncers away from us unless you want them all broken.*

"Sure thing, guys! Take your time." He leans back in his creaky chair, far enough to prop his tacky woven deck shoes onto the desk. It's all an act to make himself look calm and collected. Meanwhile, he's ready to piss in his chinos. He knows who we are. It's why his security hasn't bothered us yet. "And, hey, I've got a girl you might like to take for a spin. She's finishing up with a client, but she'll be out soon. Good girl. Top-notch. She brings in three times what my others do."

"We're not the paying type." My brother doesn't have hard limits—or any limits, for that matter—but he won't pay for a woman's attention, ever. Plus, if there's any chance this girl has so much as looked at Vic, he wouldn't touch her with a ten-foot pole.

"Oh, come on, guys. What do you take me for?" He lets out an annoying snort laugh. "Daisy's on me tonight."

"Look at this fool, peddling his dancers like they're prostitutes," Caleb murmurs wryly. But his fists are flexing. He's seconds from losing it on this weasel.

"We're not here for pussy." And this guy's a waste of our time.

"You sure?" The club owner steals another glance at Moe. "Looks like he hasn't had it in a while."

Moe takes a step forward.

I throw my hand up, stopping him in his tracks. I don't know a ton about the guy, except that he was Special Ops, he rarely utters a word, and in the three months he's been with Farley, he's edged his way up to becoming his most trusted right-hand man. As much as I might enjoy watching him work, we have far more important things to focus on than beating this kiss-ass into the cheap linoleum floor. "Start searching. If he's lying about knowing where Vic is, we can continue this chat." I offer Laney's manager a wicked smile. "I kind of hope you're lying about our cousin."

Paramedics push a gurney past us, the inmate stretched out on it letting out a low moan of pain, his hand protecting his bloody side. Did he get shanked in his bed, or was he lurking somewhere he shouldn't have been?

Because nothing good happens when you're walking around Fulcort Penitentiary at 3:00 a.m.

"You're lucky I'm working tonight." Donny turns a key. The metal door creaks open, the sound carrying along the empty corridor. It's one of a dozen gates we have to pass through to reach the inmate quarters. I'll give it to the security around here—it wouldn't be easy to break out of this place.

"Not as lucky as you are, 'cause you'd be dragging your ass here if we needed you to," I retort, trailing him. We certainly pay the guard enough money to have him at our beck and call. Of course, visits like this always cost extra, to get the staff who aren't on our payroll out of the way.

Caleb saunters behind us as if he doesn't have a care in the world. I know it's all an act. My brother is vibrating with pent-up frustration and rage. We're oh for two tonight. First, Uncle Peter's house, then Laney's was a bust, too. We scoured every corner and closet of that seedy place. The only surprise waiting for us was a happy ending for some wrinkly dude celebrating his eightieth behind a privacy curtain, courtesy of Laney's top-notch girl, Daisy. Good for him.

But bad for us, because now we're meeting our father with nothing to show for our efforts besides a flaming plane and four bodies and our thumbs up our asses.

"How'd the old man take his wake-up call?" I ask.

"You'll have to ask the newbie I sent in there." Donny

chuckles. "He should be done getting stitched up in the infirmary soon."

I shake my head. Anyone else would be eating through a straw for laying a hand on a guard. But Vlad Easton will get away with it. What's worse is the fucker thinks it's because people respect him. *No, Dad. That's not respect. They just like money under their mattress and their loved ones breathing, is all.*

Donny stops at a heavy metal door. "You've got ten minutes. Anything longer than that'll create chatter, and we have a few new guards around here."

"Ten minutes too long...," Caleb mutters, shoving through the door. It swings open with a groan. "And there's the man of the hour. Have I told you how good you look in orange?" he announces cheerfully.

Our father's face is twisted with rage—whether at his son's mocking words or at being dragged out of his cell at this hour, I can't tell. Probably both.

For fucks' sakes, Caleb.

From the corner of my eye, I catch Donny's smirk as I'm passing through, but he's smart enough to school his expression by the time I've turned to meet his gaze. "Get three more guys down here. If you hear a knock on this door, you bust in here and pull them apart," I say quietly. The last thing we need tonight is another dead body.

Donny salutes and is off, charging down the hall to corral a few trusted men.

"At least Gabriel has the decency to wait until a reasonable hour to pester me. I should have known you had something to do with this shit," Dad growls from his seat in a hard plastic chair. We're in a private room, reserved for inmates meeting with their legal counsel. Cameras in the corner are angled at the center of the room to capture shady lawyers slipping shit to their clients. Now though, the red indicator lights are off. There will be no recording any of this meeting. It's amazing what those green bills can buy around here.

"So good to see you again, Pops. And after *so* long," Caleb croons, tossing a new burner phone on the table, to replace the last one we delivered, that Dad's had long enough to assume it's been compromised.

Dad shifts, looking ready to pounce. If Caleb keeps up this antagonizing, there won't be any conversation. He'll just attack. He's surprisingly agile, despite his age and out-of-shape form.

"Someone's put a hit out on us," I quickly interject.

That grabs his attention.

I give him a run-through of the details from the night.

Dad's wrinkled forehead settles into his palms as he listens.

"We think it's Uncle Peter and Vic—"

"You *think*, dumbass!" His gruff voice booms in the tiny room. It's funny, even given his predicament—a prisoner, while we're free as birds—my stomach clenches with tension at being scolded by my father. "That son of a bitch sold me out. *Of course* it was him. And now he's trying to get rid of my bloodline. Soon, he'll have everything he wants."

"We haven't been able to track any of them down to confirm. The house is dark. No word on Vic at Laney's. Plus, they've got eyes on the deli and the dry cleaner, probably so we don't torch them. We drove by on our way here."

Caleb straddles the chair across the table from Dad, his arms nonchalantly resting across the back, as if this is a casual conversation. "Is there a reason they've gone to ground?"

Dad leans back in his chair, folding his arms across his girth. It creaks beneath his weight. "You mean, besides knowing that he's a dead man walking?"

Caleb exchanges glances with me. I guess that answers the question of whether our father has gone on the offensive. We were wrong about the heads-up. "Did you think that maybe you could have warned us before you set Bane on him?"

"What for?"

"Oh, gee, *I don't know...* so your bloodline might get some additional protection? Seeing as we don't have all these guards and walls to protect us." Caleb waves a hand around the room.

"You think *this* is *protection*?" Dad snaps. "I'm a sitting duck in here. And don't play dumb. As if you didn't know what would happen when you handed me that photograph of my brother's betrayal."

Fair enough. We did know he wouldn't sit too long and retribution would be harsh. "So what do you want us to do now?" I ask, trying to be the one with the level head.

"What I've *always* wanted you to do. What I've been grooming you to do for years. Take over Harriet."

Caleb's eyebrow arches. We expected this. Dad's been relentless in his push for us to get more involved in the Easton drug empire. "And what about Peter—"

"Peter is no longer family!" Dad barks, his face twisted in a sneer. "He has proven he can't be trusted, so the family business is now ours, one hundred percent. Don't worry about him. You go and meet with the Perris to sort out this mutual issue with our southern *friends.* And then? Make sure our supply and distribution chains are moving smoothly. Let everyone know we are in charge."

We?

Sounds more like *he* is in charge.

"Don't worry about Peter. Just like that, huh? While he's actively trying to kill us." Caleb smirks. "Where's the fatherly love?"

"Oh, you want your head rubbed? Your hair stroked?" Dad says with mock concern. "Go find one of your whores to do it. Just keep your fucking eyes open and no one can kill you. It's up to you two to keep our family legacy alive. I can't do it on my own, not from in here."

I exchange another lightning-quick glance with Caleb to see he's of the same mind. Neither of us have any interest in Dad's legacy, and the stubborn bull will refuse to accept that until his dying breath. "Peter won't take this lying down."

Dad scowls. "Bane will make sure he and those lecherous sons of his burn for what they've done, and soon."

Who knows if Vic and Alexei have any idea that their father has the FBI on speed dial? Vic's a loudmouth, and Peter knows it. Would he risk telling him? And Alexei is merely his yes man. An optional cog in the wheel. Either way, if Dad so much as suspects they've wronged him, which he clearly does, they're as good as dead and probably not in a neat and tidy way. His go-to guy, Bane—a wiry bastard with calculating eyes who has no code when it comes to who he kills—takes sick pleasure in his assignments. I've only met the guy once, but once was enough to know I don't ever want to cross paths with him again. Rumor has it that whoever dragged the tip of the blade that sliced open the side of his face ended up being fileted.

While still alive.

"You will become who I raised you to be." Dad slaps the table with his meaty palm. "It's time you two started acting like Vladimir Easton's sons and not a bunch of idiot play-boys. And why have I been hearing about some useless shmuck we're protecting in here? This Wheeler inmate. What is that about?"

Shit. I expected Dad to hear about that sooner or later, but the last thing I need is him sniffing around Mercy's father when he's spiraling with anger. "It's nothing. Just pussy."

Caleb flashes me a warning look—to keep my mouth shut—before steering a shit-eating grin our father's way. "This idiot playboy enjoys his life. At least my group showers involve the kind of ass I like."

That has the desired effect of distraction. Dad sneers with disgust. "Your mother would be rolling in her grave at the man you've become."

Oh fuck. Here we go.

My brother's dark blue eyes flare with rage. Mentioning Mom in her grave to him is *never* a good idea, and Dad knows it. He only does it when he's looking for a fight.

I move fast for the door, my fist banging hard.

"OLD MAN still has a mean right hook, I'll give him that." Caleb tests his split lip with his finger, pulling away to find fresh blood. His left eye is already swelling.

I shake my head. It took all four guards to pull those two apart. They moved fast, giving Caleb time for only a few shots. They were good ones though. Dad's not going to enjoy eating his meals for a few days on account of a sore jaw. Thankfully, Dad welcomes aggression in his sons, otherwise we'd have to worry about *both* pillars of the Easton empire putting hits out on us.

On the plus side, Caleb successfully steered Dad away

from the topic of Mercy and providing her father protection. The less he knows, the better.

"Sounds like this is unfolding even better than we hoped." Caleb's voice is low as he eyes Donny, ten feet ahead of us.

"Better?" I snort. "You were hoping someone would blow up our plane with us *in it*?"

"Nah. I mean, Dad's taking care of *all* the loose ends for us."

I frown at my brother, not understanding.

"You trust Vic or Alexei to keep their mouths shut if they were backed in a corner by the Feds?"

"No," I admit. Vic would squeal like a piglet with its foot trapped the second Special Agent Jim DeShaw glanced his way. He'd probably give them enough intel to shut Empire down and tear it to shreds, looking for hard evidence.

We knew Dad would sic Bane on Uncle Peter. With him gone, our cousins would take over. But Dad's not going to be satisfied with just his brother's head; all their heads are on the chopping block. Dad thinks he's doing us a huge favor, securing the dirty drug business that we don't want for our futures. He expects us to step in, and he won't stop until we do. Or he's dead.

And this is where our alliance with Merrick and Vince Perri comes into play for our benefit. That we're helping orchestrate a chain reaction that will eliminate our own father still doesn't sit well with me, but it's not like we're giving the kill order. We're merely puppet masters pulling strings, not triggers. That's what I need to keep telling myself to get through this.

And it's the only way Caleb and I will get to live our lives. If Vlad has his way, we'll be rotting behind these same walls long after he's died of old age. *If* someone doesn't kill us, that is.

But with this plan we've concocted with the two younger Perris, we'll be out of the dirty drug business for good. Leo Perri and the cartel can battle over territory until they kill each other.

"Can you believe he actually had the nerve to bring up Mom?" Caleb shakes his head, his fists clenching. "It's his fucking fault she's gone in the first place."

"He's never seen it that way." The blame has always landed squarely on Camillo Perri's shoulders.

"It'll *always* be that way, for *any* woman crazy enough to get involved with us. Why do you think I won't ever settle down?"

"Because you're afraid your dick will fall off if it's in the same woman two days in a row?" I tease. Meanwhile, I can't help but think about Mercy. She's innocent. *More* innocent than our mother even, who chose to marry Dad knowing what he was. Mercy didn't choose this life. She would have happily spat in my face at the start, only I dangled something she couldn't resist in front of her and lured her in.

And now... now, something real is happening between us that I sure as shit never expected.

But she almost died tonight. *I* almost got her killed. That's a reality that's sitting heavily on my shoulders, one I'm unable to shrug off.

One that scares the shit out of me more than any threat to myself or even Caleb. There's no way Uncle Peter knows about her yet. Sure, he might hear that two women were traveling with us, but he'll assume they're just the flavor of the week, to be replaced or swapped out. Nameless fucks. He'll never guess that the woman sharing my bed lately actually means something to me.

If I were a decent guy, I'd tell her to pack her shit and leave tonight and never look in my direction again.

Too bad I'm not a decent guy. I'm a selfish asshole who can't stand the idea of not waking to that floral smell on my pillow and the feel of her warm, soft skin pressed against mine.

What I *can* do is make sure no one harms a single silky strand of hair on her head. I won't let her out of my sight until this shit gets sorted.

Donny walks us out the last gate. "The big guy mentioned needing extra protection. He wants guards assigned."

I meet Caleb's flat gaze. Dad wants protection from Uncle Peter. That's something we weren't anticipating in this little plan of ours. More eyes on Dad means Camillo will have a harder time reaching him after we've dealt with Miles, and this plan won't come full circle.

But if we don't give the illusion that we care about Dad's safety, he'll grow suspicious.

I sigh. "An extra guy might be a good idea."

"You got it, boss."

"And I want to know about any visitors or messages coming through for him." A new burner phone means his contacts don't have his number unless he specifically sends it to them.

"I'll do my best. Fight next week still on?"

"If Chops is up to it. Keep an eye on him for me." I hand the guard another wad of cash, which he accepts with a nod and a covert glance around, and then I'm digging the keys for the Lincoln out of my pocket. "Tell me we're done for the night?" My adrenaline is finally waning. Staying awake for the drive home will be a challenge.

"Yeah. I need ice and a few hours' sleep." Caleb checks

his eye in the mirror and curses under his breath. "Look what the bastard did to this handsome face."

I smirk. "I'm sure Michelle won't complain."

"Shit, is that her name? I think I called her Meghan."

I roll my eyes. "What are we doing about Peter?"

He sighs heavily, slapping the sunshade back in place. "Bane will catch up with him. There's nowhere you can hide from that devil. Meanwhile, we drive to Vegas and make that fucking asshole think we're good, obedient sons and everything's going according to plan."

It is.

Just not Vlad Easton's plan.

FIVE
MERCY

I WAKE to a fingertip skating across my cheek and jolt.

"Shhh," Gabriel murmurs, smiling down at me. "It's just me."

"What time is it?" I ask, my voice full of sleep, my head smoggy with lingering scotch. I'm curled up in a lounge chair. The inky dark sky has been replaced with a predawn pinkish hue.

"Late. Or early, take your pick." He brushes hair off my forehead.

Last night's events hit me in a wave then—the explosion, the squad of armed security guards circling us, Gabriel and Caleb heading out the door for retribution—and heaviness swiftly settles on my chest. Michelle and I hid by the lap pool outside Gabriel's room, where it felt more private. I didn't expect to fall asleep, but I obviously did.

I check the lounge chair next to me to find it empty.

"Caleb carried her to his room," Gabriel confirms.

"What happened? Is everything okay?" My fingertips search Gabriel's forearms, his biceps, his shoulders, his cheeks, testing for injuries. I see nothing—no bruised knuckles, no drops of blood. Nothing that mars Gabriel's perfection aside from heavy bags beneath his eyes. I sigh with relief.

He smirks, as if my doting reaction is amusing. "I'm fine."

"And Caleb?" I can't believe I'm giving that jerk a second's thought.

"He's fine. Everything's fine." He tugs at the tie on my robe, loosening it, allowing him to push the terry cloth sides apart to reveal the black string bikini I slipped on in case we decided to go for a swim. He reaches for a triangle cup, dragging it aside to uncover a breast.

"Gabriel." I press my hand against his, stalling it while covering myself. "The security guys—"

"Are out front. The camera is off. Don't worry, I want them to see this less than you do." He shakes my grip off and dips down to suck my nipple into his mouth.

He knows my feelings about spectators, but I can tell how much he needs this right now. Besides, my body is already welcoming his attention. I cradle his head of silky sandy-brown hair in my arms as his tongue lingers over my flesh. "Are we safe now?"

He pauses his teasing. "You'll be safe as long as you're with me."

"Are you sure about that?" I was with him last night when we almost died. It seems that as long as I'm with Gabriel, I'm more likely to be in grave danger.

He lifts his gaze to stare intently at me, and in his eyes I see something I can't read. "I will *never* let anyone hurt you. They'll die for even trying. Do you understand?"

I swallow and nod. *What have you done, Gabriel?* I know what he's capable of doing or ordering to have done. The man who tormented my father behind bars—the reason

I found myself living under this roof and sleeping in Gabriel's bed in the first place—is proof of that. Apparent suicide while in solitary confinement. No one is buying that story, but no one is talking. The worst part? I'm happy that guy is dead. He beat my father to near death. He was going to kill him, eventually. As far as I'm concerned, he got what he deserved. So did Fleet, the guy who tried to rape me, who my father unintentionally killed.

What do these types of convictions say about me though?

Maybe I'm no better than Gabriel. Maybe I belong with a man as jaded as he is.

Especially when I'm looking at him now and am less repulsed by the violence and more enamored with how far he'll go to protect me.

I don't argue when Gabriel pushes aside the other cup of my bikini top and yanks on the strings around my hips, loosening the bottoms until they're nothing more than a scrap of material that he tugs and flings aside. His dark gaze roams my naked flesh as the first glimmer of sun crests over the horizon, bathing the valley in a beam of light, and I feel my body flooding with warmth and anticipation.

But instead of his words turning dirty and his hands and mouth venturing between my legs as they routinely do without delay, he stretches his heavy body alongside mine on the chair and lays a languid kiss against my lips, that turns into another, and another, his thumb stroking my cheek with affection. It's unlike his usual demeanor. It's... tender.

I'm dismayed when he breaks free, but he isn't leaving. He maneuvers to slide his arm beneath my shoulders and pull me into him. I end up half-draped across his body, my face nuzzled against his neck, inhaling the faint lingering scent of his cologne. "I'm sorry to put you through all of this," he murmurs, stroking my jawline.

"It's not your fault," I say without thought. Maybe it is, though? What has Gabriel done to earn this kind of wrath? And what has inspired an apology from him in the first place? He's never apologized for anything else he's put me through up until now, and he certainly has sins to atone for. "I'm sorry about your friends." I already offered that last night, but I feel the need to say it again.

His broad chest heaves with a sigh. "Yeah. Me too," he says, his voice suddenly gruff.

We lie quietly in each other's arms, Gabriel seemingly content to watch the rising sun, his eyelids suddenly heavy with sleep, looking moments from drifting off.

This moment right here, this side of Gabriel... I could get used to this.

I burrow my face deeper into his neck, dragging my tongue along his hot skin to steal a taste of him. "I was really looking forward to going to Vegas with you," I finally admit in a near-whisper, as if it's sacrilegious to say such a thing given the people who died last night. But I've never been, and I was excited to celebrate finishing my degree after years of night classes year-round. I was excited to *finally* have something in my life to celebrate.

"Good, because we're still going."

"*Seriously?*" My stomach clenches at the thought of returning to that tarmac. Will the charred plane still be there? "Gabriel, I don't think I can handle flying—"

"We're driving. It's only four hours away."

"Oh." I pause. "When?"

"We're leaving within the hour."

I laugh. "I guess I'm driving, then? Seeing as you can barely keep your eyes open." Caleb can't be much better.

"Farley's driving. I'll sleep on the way." He smirks. "Caleb'll sleep when he's dead."

He's joking, but his words trigger another, more serious thought. "We're taking those security guys with us to Vegas?"

"Yeah." A pause and then I feel his body grow suddenly tense beneath me. "Why? Did something happen last night?" His voice is hard. "Did one of them try something—"

"No, no! Nothing like that." They barely spared us a glance, that we were aware of, anyway. But bringing a security detail with us all the way to Vegas can only mean one thing. A sinking feeling stirs in the pit of my stomach. I pull away, angling myself so I can see his face and he can see mine. "Whoever blew up the plane last night is still out there, aren't they?" The threat hasn't been resolved after all.

"It's fine," he begins to say, shrugging my worry off.

"It's not fine, Gabriel. None of this is fine! Or normal." I don't mean to sound shrill. But what if this is normal in Gabriel's world? What if it's only matter of time before they succeed? "Who's doing this? Who's threatening you?"

A muscle in Gabriel's jaw ticks. "My uncle Peter."

My mouth hangs open for a beat. I didn't expect him to actually tell me the truth. "Your *uncle* is trying to kill you? As in, your own family?" He mentioned an uncle once, when I asked if it was just him and Caleb. An uncle and a few cousins, he had said, growing edgy at their mention. Now I see why.

He sighs heavily. "My uncle is the one who put my father in jail. The snake was working with the Feds."

"Why?" Besides the fact that Gabriel's father deserves to be behind bars. But isn't there a code between criminals?

And he's definitely a criminal—he murdered four people last night!

"So he could take over the family business. Take a hundred percent of the profit."

"The family business." I level Gabriel with a steady look. We're getting dangerously close to discussing things he said he couldn't discuss. "You don't mean Empire, do you?"

He regards me a long moment before shaking his head once. "He can have it, for all Caleb and I care. We don't want it."

"So then let him have it—"

"It's not that simple. My father is—" His lips twist. "—determined that we follow in his footsteps. He found out about my uncle's betrayal recently, and needless to say, he wasn't happy."

A memory strikes me, of the hard-faced man with the pockmarks on his cheeks banging his fists against the table and storming away from Gabriel in the visitors' room at Fulcort. "You're the one who told him, aren't you?"

"The information… presented itself to us recently, yes. So I made my father aware. He needed to know who he could trust. Or not trust, is the case." Gabriel hesitates, and I hold my breath, desperate for him to keep going, though I know I'm not going to like what I hear if he does. "And then he decided that the family would be better off without certain members in it."

"You mean your uncle."

Gabriel nods. "He deserves what's coming to him. He would have been better off putting a bullet in my father's back. Be a man about it. But feeding intel to the Feds? That will earn *anyone* an automatic death sentence."

Jesus. Is Gabriel admitting to his father putting a hit out on someone? Suddenly I wish he hadn't told me, but it's too late.

"Peter caught wind of the hit out on him. He and his family have gone into hiding."

"Until when?" A moment later, I answer the question for myself. "Until you and Caleb and your dad are dead. Oh my God." A cold dread washes over me. What kind of family have I gotten myself involved with?

"He won't show his face until we're taken care of." He adds more softly, "Like the bunch of damn cowards that they are."

"So then, maybe it'd be smarter if *we* stayed put here while all this is happening?" In a gated community on top of a mountain, with several acres surrounding us and cameras angled at every corner coming in? Sounds a lot safer than the Vegas Strip at the moment.

"Fuck that. We don't hide," he growls. "Besides, we have important business to take care of. I don't want to miss this opportunity." He rubs my shoulder. "But you're not leaving my side unless it's necessary, and when you do, you'll have Moe with you at all times. He's the best of Farley's guys. He's highly trained. No one will get to you with him there, I promise."

"For how long?"

"Until this is sorted out. Days... weeks...." He looks like he wants to say more, but he stops himself.

I begin processing. "I can't show up at Mary's Way with a security guard." They rarely let men into the building, and not the kind of guys I spied last night—juiced-up military-grade goons armed with multiple guns.

Gabriel chuckles, but there's no humor in the sound. "You're not going to work while this is going on."

"Gabriel, I can't just *not* go to work."

"You don't have a choice. You're not going." There's an edge to his voice.

"And what am I supposed to tell my boss?" I sputter.

"That you're working from home, that you're sick with the plague; I don't give a fuck what you say, but you're not going there until I know you'll be safe, and that's nonnegotiable."

"We may have an arrangement but you don't own me," I snap, irritated. I begin to push away, intent on leaving him there on the lounge chair.

His arms tighten around me, holding me in place. "Did you forget that I bought you your job, Mercy? You were going to resign because they couldn't afford you anymore. I paid a hundred grand so you could keep going down to that shithole every day. I think that's bought you some goddamn time off."

I should have known there'd be strings attached to the anonymous donation he made.

"Go fuck yourself." I dig my elbow into the hard pad of muscle covering his ribs.

Gabriel's answering grin is wicked with intent. "I'd rather fuck you." His lips land on mine.

I respond by biting his bottom lip—not to hurt him, but to let him know I'm pissed.

When he pulls back, when I see the flare of heat in his stormy blue eyes, I know the soft side of Gabriel is gone, replaced by a version I'm coming to enjoy as much. Our argument is not over—we'll pick that up again later—but for now I'm content to watch him stand and shed his clothes, my inner muscles clenching in anticipation at the sight of his beautiful, muscular body and his swollen length.

He straddles the lounge chair and, seizing my thighs, drags my limber body down to meet his.

I let out a content moan as I feel him entering me, stretching my body wide under the morning sky.

"You're going to buy *this*?" Michelle's emerald green eyes widen as she presses her forehead against the SUV's passenger seat window to take in the impressive Mage Hotel and Casino towering above us. She and Caleb took the middle row, while Gabriel and I curled into the back, both of us stealing a few hours of sleep.

"Possibly." Caleb smirks, amused by her awe, but it falls off quickly and is replaced by a wince. While Gabriel returned unscathed, I can't say the same for his older brother, who looks like he got pummeled. The bruises across his knuckles hint that some unlucky bastard got as good as he gave. "Except the owner doesn't know he's selling it to us yet."

I frown at Gabriel. What does that mean? Do I want to know?

He answers with a bored yawn and an eye rub, having stirred from slumber ten minutes ago.

"I came here the last time I was in Vegas. It's *really* nice inside. They have a Cirque show here," Michelle murmurs, absently toying with the diamond necklace adorning her neck—stock from her father's Scottsdale jewelry store. "Will you change the name?"

"Yeah. Definitely. Vegas needs an Empire."

Her eyes sparkle as she finally peels away from the view to smile at Caleb, reaching across the seat to give his thigh a friendly stroke. "Like the nightclub."

He winks with his good eye. "Just like it."

I don't know what's going on between these two, but it

won't end well. Michelle's not the type to share, and I know enough about Caleb to know he's not a one-pussy kind of man.

Selfishly though, I'm relieved Michelle agreed to make the trip to Vegas with us, even if it ends with her crying on my shoulder over what an asshole Gabriel's brother is after she catches him with a woman or three.

The black SUV ahead of us, carrying a carload of Farley's goons—I should stop thinking of them like that, they're here to keep us safe—pulls up to the covered entrance. They pile out in unison, setting the elegantly dressed doormen into motion. These guys must see guests arriving with security details on the regular. This is Vegas, after all, and from what I can see of the staff uniforms and multiple water fountains and landscaping, this is a high-end hotel that people with money frequent.

Farley's men don't look like regular security guys, though. They look like they're ready for war, clad in head-to-toe black, with bulletproof vests and multiple guns strapped to their bodies, and earpieces to exchange codes and commands.

Farley watches them disappear into the hotel. After a few long moments, he and Moe, the guy in the passenger side—the smallest of them all but with a crazed look in his eyes that makes me nervous and his otherwise attractive features seem less so—must receive the all clear, because they pull in and unlock the doors for us to pile out.

Michelle might have been gaping at the exterior, but I'm the one struggling to keep my jaw from hanging as our entourage strolls through the glass doors and into frigid temps, a shock in comparison to the dry heat of the desert in midday August. The grand foyer is a vacuous white marble-clad space that stretches several stories tall.

Multiple elaborate water fountains grace the center, creating a divide.

"You're going to buy *this*?" I hear myself echo Michelle's earlier words. How can a person afford such a place?

"Maybe," Gabriel murmurs, low enough for only me to hear. "We've got it on good authority that it'll be up for sale soon at a good price."

"A good price?" I blink at him. "Like the-GDP-of-a-small-country good price?"

Gabriel chuckles and slips his arm around my waist, pulling me into his side possessively, pressing a kiss against my temple.

I find myself leaning into his lips instinctively, closing my eyes as I revel in the feel of his mouth against my skin. They've become familiar lips; a skilled mouth that has proven far more gentle than I ever expected.

When I open my eyes, Caleb is watching us, a knowing grin curling the good side of his face.

Others are watching, too—couples strolling hand in hand; groups of friends loitering in the lobby, in Vegas with high hopes for creating wild once-in-a-lifetime memories. What must we look like to outsiders looking in? They certainly can't see the twisted arrangement that got me here. I'll bet we look like a regular, loving couple, and while people might guess that these two handsome men have wealth, they wouldn't suspect that they're basically mob royalty. They certainly wouldn't guess that the four of us nearly died last night.

A reality that I'm still numb to as I saunter along.

An attractive blond woman in a stylish white suit exchanges words with the doorman who received us and then marches this way, her spiky heels clicking with steady ease against the marble. "Welcome to the Mage, Mr. Green. I'll be happy to show you to your suite," she says in a crisp voice, offering Caleb a polite albeit stiff smile.

It catches me off guard. I'm not used to seeing a female *not* fawn over the man. His face isn't *that* mangled.

And *Mr. Green*? I flash a questioning look Gabriel's way.

He leans in to kiss a spot on my neck beneath my ear that sends shivers radiating through my body. "We never check in using our real names, especially not around here."

"He couldn't be more creative?"

"He likes that one. Green, like money."

I shouldn't be surprised. "And who are you?"

"Someone idiotic, no doubt. It's Caleb's thing, and he likes to have fun with it." He sounds unbothered.

As if on cue, the woman turns to us, her attention on Gabriel. A small gold pin on her lapel reads Sienna. A complementary black one below marks her as a manager. "Mr. Pink Panther?"

I snort, earning a pinch against my side.

Gabriel smirks. "Sure."

Her face doesn't so much as crack, the epitome of professionalism, though she must know that's a fake name. Even a halfwit would figure that out. "Welcome to the Mage. I hope you enjoy your stay."

Gabriel dips his head. "So do we."

She affords him a lingering look and then shifts her focus to lead us toward the elevator, fumbling for the key card that dangles from a lanyard around her neck. She hasn't spared so much as a glance for me, I note. It's as if I don't even exist.

"What's wrong?" Gabriel asks.

I realize I'm scowling. "How does she know I'm not *Mrs*. Pink Panther?"

His eyebrows pop. "You *want* to be Mrs. *Pink* Panther?"

"No! But I would like to at least be acknowledged—"

"Because we've come to the right place for you to become Mrs. Pink Panther."

"No, I do *not* want that," I say more firmly than I intend.

"Why not?" he asks, a hint of genuine curiosity in his voice.

It's my turn to raise my eyebrows at him. "Are you kidding me? Let me count the reasons." He coerced me into this relationship, his mob boss father is in prison, his uncle is trying to kill him, and he's about to buy this hotel with drug money. If I wasn't here, he'd probably screw Sienna before dinner. He's so far from marriage material, it's almost laughable.

"Fair enough," he murmurs as we pile into an elevator that's marked directly for the top floor penthouse. It's a smooth, quick ascent, and silent until we reach the top.

"This elevator is yours for the duration of your stay. There is a service elevator behind the games room, used only by our cleaning staff. We have two levels of luxury suites, but as you will see, the penthouse comprises the full top floor of this tower. Well, technically, two floors."

The doors open, and I hear Michelle's breath hitch as we get our first look at our digs for the weekend. Her family may be wealthy, but even they wouldn't rent out a place like this.

My own eyes search the opulent textures and complementary colors—soothing tans and grays with punches of rich plum and cherry—in quiet awe. To our left is a massive living area with multiple sectional couches and flat screen

TVs. Beyond it, a wall of floor-to-ceiling glass that reveals an expansive patio and our own private pool. There is a full bar to our right, with barstool seating for ten. A winding staircase ahead leads up to, I assume, the bedrooms.

This is, as Michelle would call it, "next level." And it's probably costing equivalent to half a year of my apartment's rent per night.

"Good enough for you, Mrs. Pink Panther?" Gabriel mocks, his hand smoothing over my ass, capping it off with a squeeze.

I let him see me roll my eyes before stepping out of the elevator.

"Stay here until we clear it," Farley demands in a rumbling voice. The five men with him fan out to search the space with quick precision, guns in hand.

"I can assure you, the safety and discretion of all our guests are of utmost importance at the Mage," Sienna says, her sharp blue eyes wide as she watches them move, her rigid façade wavering with a touch of uncertainty. Does she wonder who Mr. Green and Mr. Pink Panther really are? Or does she already know? If they buy this place, will they keep the staff? Will the staff want to stay?

"We're happy to hear that," Caleb says with an easy smile, though he doesn't make a move, abiding by Farley's instruction. "Has the bar been stocked like I asked?"

She offers a curt nod. "Everything is as you wished, and if it's not, please dial your personal concierge. Her name is Daniela, and she'll be more than happy to assist you."

"Thank you..." His blue gaze shifts to her name tag, and farther, to a hint of cleavage. "Sienna."

I steal a glance at Michelle to see if she's noticed the predatory look on his face, if she recognizes it for what it is.

I've seen it before, when the girls from Empire are strolling topless around the house.

"All clear," Farley announces from the top of the stairs, sliding his gun back into his holster.

Sienna holds a french-manicured hand out. "As you will see, your private pool is—"

"We're good." Caleb cuts her off.

She purses her lips in a tight smile. "Might I show you to your bedrooms then?"

Caleb grins. "Don't worry, I always find the bedrooms just fine."

Sienna clears her throat. "Is there anything else I can help you with?"

His grin grows sly as he eyes her.

This time, Michelle doesn't miss the exchange. Her face hardens with awareness.

Thankfully, Gabriel distracts. "Can you make us spa reservations? For two guests—" Gabriel scans his Rolex. "—an hour from now? For the entire afternoon. Full service."

"Certainly." With another nod, she ducks into the elevator. Just as the doors are closing, I catch the unimpressed glare she shoots Caleb.

I decide I like that woman. Hopefully she'll tell him to fuck off when he dials up the lewd suggestions.

Gabriel moves for the bar. "Ladies, make yourself at home."

I trail him. "I never took you for a spa man."

"I'm not. You're going with Michelle. We have a meeting." He collects the tumbler of vodka Caleb just poured and holds it out to me.

I shake my head—it's noon. Michelle, however, accepts a glass with a smile. I can't begrudge her that, given what she's been through since stepping out of the SUV last night. "A meeting about buying this place?"

"Yeah." Gabriel's gaze flashes to Caleb.

He's lying, of course. I'm beginning to recognize Gabriel's tells, and one of his most obvious ones is a secretive look between him and his brother. Whatever this important meeting is, it has nothing to do with buying the Mage. But for once I'm not mad that he's being dishonest with me. I think I'd rather sink into a mud bath and play dumb to whatever these two have cooking than know.

Is that how mob wives are born?

The security team disperses—one outside, three heading for the elevator, Moe moving down a hallway where I suspect he'll find the staff elevator. Only Farley remains, stationing himself in a corner near the bar, as if trying to be unobtrusive. As if his mammoth muscular frame could blend into the shimmering wallpaper.

When will they sleep? *Where* will they sleep?

Do they even sleep?

"I could see myself getting used to this place," Caleb announces, his eye—the one that isn't swollen shut—now on the rooftop patio and pool.

"Good, because you'll be the one squatting here for the next six months while we get up and running." Gabriel's phone chirps. He slips it out of his pocket to check the screen, and I note that it's not the one he uses to call me and take business calls from Empire.

This one must be an untraceable phone for his illicit activities.

Silence hangs as he taps out a response.

"All set?" Caleb asks.

"Yup." Gabriel drops it back in his pocket.

"And we haven't decided on who's living here, yet."

Gabriel smirks. "If you say so."

Caleb throws his middle finger up at his brother before slipping the same hand into Michelle's and leading her out to the patio, as if he wasn't just ogling another woman in front of her.

And she follows, giggling as if she didn't witness the exchange.

"They're getting along well," Gabriel notes.

Too well. "If he touches that woman, or *any* woman, while we're gone and I find out, I swear to God I'll give him a matching black eye," I warn. "I'm not kidding."

Gabriel smiles through a sip. I wonder if he's recalling the time I slapped him for propositioning me in the prison parking lot. I drew blood. For a moment, I thought he would kill me. "He won't be tempted. At least, not for the afternoon. And you're taking Moe with you."

Not this again. I steal a glance to where Farley hovers, pretending to not listen. "An armed dude hovering over me at a spa? It kind of defeats the purpose of going, doesn't it?" How can I even attempt to relax?

Gabriel's sigh is heavy with forced patience. "He can wait in the lobby."

I open my mouth to argue.

"He's the best bodyguard I've got. He just wants to make sure you're safe. He'll stay out of your way." Farley's grumbling voice cut into the quiet room. "He specifically asked to be on your detail."

Moe asked to follow me around? Why the hell would he ask? Is that supposed to make me feel better?

"Mercy. *Please.* There's shit going on that you don't have any clue about." There's a tired, strained edge to Gabriel's voice that makes me feel like a spoiled brat.

I bite my tongue and nod sullenly.

"Should I have the mud bath or the rejuvenating massage?" Michelle muses, studying the menu card.

Amie, the hostess behind the counter, a pristinely manicured blond dressed in a white suit much like Sienna's, flashes a toothy smile. "Why not both?"

"Why not, *indeed*." Michelle giggles and turns her attention to me. "Seeing as we're not paying for any of this… what are you in the mood for?"

I roll my shoulders in a poor attempt to remove the soreness from sleeping in the lounge chair by the pool last night. "Lying on a table while someone pampers me for hours?" The Mage spa looks more than equipped to handle that task. I was a little wary to commit myself to an entire afternoon here, but the moment we stepped through the doors and I inhaled the rosewater scent lingering in the air and took in the expanse of cool gray marble, a calming sense washed over me. I've never had a real massage—one by a professional and that didn't equate to foreplay—and now I'm in no rush to leave.

But I can't ignore the voice in the back of my mind that keeps reminding me which business is footing the bill for the luxury we're afforded this weekend. Is it wrong to lavish in it if we're simply recipients?

It was one thing for Mary's Way to unintentionally accept a hundred thousand dollar check. A twisted irony of sorts—that the money Marsha will be using to fix all of the rehab center's leaks and creaks and shortcomings so we can continue accepting drug addicts is coming from the very business that created those drug addicts.

But at least in that case, Gabriel's money is going to a good cause.

Now, it's going to silky smooth skin and fewer muscle knots.

"We have the two-hour or the three-hour personalized rejuvenation massage sessions to choose from." Amie taps the menu card with the tip of her pen, and I try not to balk at the price tags listed next to each line item. "Why don't you do the three-hour, while your friend can start with a mud bath and whirlpool and then do the two-hour."

"Perf!" Michelle squeals. Clearly she's not battling with the same moral demons as I am.

"It's settled then. Let me take you to your rooms, ladies." Amie comes around the desk to lead us farther into the spa.

Moe, who I did my best to ignore while he hovered by the glass entrance door, closes the distance to sidle up behind me.

Amie eyes him warily. "Will... he be joining you in the treatment room?"

I sigh in an attempt to expel my annoyance. "He'll just check everything out and then he'll wait out here for us." Visually dissecting every person who enters for signs of a threat, no doubt. I wish Gabriel had sent Farley instead. He might be the size of a grizzly bear, but at least he doesn't have the crazy eyes.

Amie's smile is tight as she leads us down the hall, and I think I catch her muttering "Fun times" under her breath.

I COULD GET USED to this.

The soft notes of a flute tickle my eardrum as I lie in my cocoon on the table, my eyes shuttered with a cooling face mask. The aesthetician scrubbed my body and slathered it with what she called a "cocoa-rich formula" before wrapping me in plastic. She then ducked out, telling me she'd be back in a half hour and to simply relax and enjoy the quiet while my skin absorbs the medley of serums and creams.

At first, thirty minutes—bound and unable to move, to check my phone, to do *anything*—sounded like an eternity. But between the music and the dim lights and the heavenly chocolate scent seeping into my body, I feel the tension slipping from my muscles as each minute passes.

I've nearly drifted off when the slightest creak of the door announces her reentry.

"Feel good?" she asks softly.

I make a humming sound of contentment, the effort to form actual words too much.

"I've heard Gabriel Easton doesn't spare any expense for his women."

All the calm from the past hour evaporates as my body goes rigid. I never mentioned Gabriel, and that voice doesn't match the aesthetician's. Hers was wispy. This one is deep and commanding.

I open my mouth to scream for Moe—I can't move, bound in plastic as I am—when the eye mask is peeled from my face.

"Relax. I'm not here to hurt you," the woman says. "I just want to talk."

It takes a few blinks and moments for my eyesight to return in the dimly lit room. I focus on the woman who stands over me in a spa robe, her thick mane of curly black hair held back by a white headband, her brown skin radiant, as if she just left a facial—only the swipe of plum eyeshadow across her lids denies that. She smiles easily, but behind that smile and those striking coffee-colored eyes, I see calculation. She has me cornered, and we both know it.

"Who are you?" I ask, though I think I already have an idea.

"My name is Special Agent Kennedy Lewis of the FBI. Call me Kennedy. And you're Mercy Wheeler."

Holy shit. I swallow against the swell of panic that surges. The FBI knows *my name.* I mean, my name was taken down last night by law enforcement people after the explosion, but I assumed it was strictly for report purposes.

And now the FBI is in my spa treatment room.

In Vegas.

Have I become a face on a board in a room somewhere? Is there a line drawn from the Easton crime family to me? I *know* this is about Gabriel. Who else could it be about? My father is the only other supposed criminal in my life, and he's behind bars.

"Does the FBI normally sneak into private spa rooms?" I ask, failing to keep the shake from my voice.

Kennedy's smile widens. "We do what we must, especially when there's a rather intimidating man standing at the entrance to the spa, scaring everyone." She seems amused by Moe.

"My aesthetician will be back any minute—"

"My partner's keeping her busy. But you're right, we don't have a lot of time, so let's get right down to it."

You haven't done anything wrong, I remind myself as I take a calming breath. "Okay? What do you want to talk about?"

"Your boyfriend, Gabriel Easton."

"He's not my—" I begin to say but cut myself off. It's probably better the Feds think we're in a relationship rather than know about our arrangement and the bank account at my disposal. "Why do you want to know about him?"

"Let's call him a person of interest in an investigation," she says casually. "How'd you two meet?"

"I can't remember," I say, my mind spinning to formulate a lie. But *why* am I lying? There's nothing illegal about the way we met.

"Was it at Fulcort? Both of your fathers are serving time there. It stands to reason," she presses.

Stupid Mercy. Of course the FBI would have done a preliminary search to learn some specifics about me. I'll bet Dad's status was near the top of "facts about Mercy." "Yeah. A few weeks after my father began his sentence. I... ran into him in the parking lot. I thought he was attractive." *Please ignore any surveillance footage that might have captured me slapping him, suggesting otherwise.*

"Do you know how he and his brother make their money?" Her eyes narrow, and I feel like a bug on a magnifying glass with her hovering over me.

"They own Empire?" It comes out as a question. I clear my throat to add, "It's a nightclub."

Kennedy's head cocks as she studies me for a long moment. "You're a college student, aren't you?"

"Not anymore. I wrote my last exam yesterday."

"Congratulations." She smiles. "And you work at Mary's Way. You've been there for six... seven years?"

"Six. I'm training to be a counselor."

"For *drug addiction.*" Her perfectly drawn eyebrow arches as she emphasizes those words, and I catch a hint of amusement. Not because it's funny, but because of the irony, I gather.

They know so much about me already.

They *definitely* have my face on a bulletin board.

She begins to pace. "You're a smart girl. Do you *really*

believe those two make that much money running a nightclub?"

"It's a *really* nice club. High end," I croak, my eyes darting to the door as I pray for Anna the aesthetician to magically appear.

She opens her mouth to speak but hesitates, as if changing her mind. "So, what are you guys doing in Vegas?" She's taken on a casual tone.

"Like I said, I just finished school. Gabriel offered to bring me and my best friend here to celebrate. I've never been." Have they snuck into Michelle's room to interrogate her, yet?

"You've been working on that degree for a while, too, haven't you?"

A cold unease slides down my spine. Special Agent Kennedy Lewis knows *a lot* about me.

"Any other reason? Anything you might have overheard?"

Like that they're planning on buying this hotel? I'd like to think they're not going to do anything illegal to make the deal go through, but who knows with those two? I err on the side of caution and shake my head.

"Nothing at all—"

"No," I say, a little too forcefully. "Like I said, we're here to celebrate. It's taken me a few extra years to finish my degree. I've had a lot going on in my life lately."

Kennedy's gaze searches the empty walls, silent for a moment. "How is your father doing?"

I blink several times, processing the sudden subject change. "As well as to be expected."

She nods slowly. "But better than he was, from what I hear. That Diego Montoya guy really did a number on him a few weeks ago. Before Diego was murdered in solitary."

I swallow against the rising panic. "I heard he committed suicide."

Kennedy makes a doubtful sound. "Right. And your father intended to kill his coworker. What was his name again? Fleet?"

"He didn't!" My anger sparks.

"Exactly." Kennedy circles my table slowly. "He shouldn't be in there for murder, especially after what that guy tried to do to you."

It's the first time anyone with any authoritative power has admitted that to me. "Right."

"But it seems he's made some friends on the inside. They're protecting him."

"He's a likeable guy."

"Still... it's got to be hard for you. Dad, in prison for the next few decades. Mom, deceased years ago. Drug overdose."

"Yeah. It is." And that's the truth.

Her smile wavers. "The Easton family has been a key player in the heroin and cocaine drug trade for several decades now. *Everything* they buy—the cars, the house, the money for you to lie here enveloped like this"—her hand waves aimlessly over me—"has been bought and paid for by the sales of drugs." She watches me carefully, looking for a reaction. Or a lack thereof, if she suspects this isn't news to me.

"You're wrong," I hear myself say, because denial seems to be the best option.

"I'm not wrong, Mercy. I wish I were, for your sake. I can't imagine you'd *choose* to be carrying on with a man like that, given your career choice and history with your mother."

I didn't choose this! I want to yell. Had the system not so spectacularly failed my father, I never would have met Gabriel Easton. I never would have appeared on his radar. He never would have had the opportunity to play on my desperation.

And now? Somehow I'm at a spa in Vegas and I seem to have lost sight of all the reasons Gabriel is not a man I'd ever want.

If she senses my inner turmoil, she doesn't let on. "The Easton family has enemies. A lot of them. And the longer you're with him, the more likely you are to get dragged down into his world. Look what happened last night. You almost died."

"That was a fuel leak," I mumble.

"Is that what he told you? Is that why you have a bodyguard out there? Because of a fuel leak?" She smirks, but it falls off immediately. "Did you know his mother died?"

"He mentioned it."

"Did he mention *how* she died?" She drifts around the table, studying me with an arched brow.

Have the FBI checked my internet searches at work? If they have, they'd know that I've combed through countless news articles about Vlad Easton and his murdered bride already.

I say nothing—not lying, not admitting. It seems like the safest answer.

It prompts Kennedy to continue. "She was killed by a rival family. I'll leave the details out for now, but suffice it to say it wasn't a quick or pleasant end." She furrows her brow. "I would hate to see the same thing happen to you. But you can help us stop the Easton family from destroying more families and more lives. You'd want to do that, wouldn't you?"

She pauses a moment, waiting for my answer.

I wait quietly for her to continue.

"Sometimes these guys get careless, especially around the women they share a bed with. He might start answering phone calls around you or entertaining business partners at his club while you're there. He might have a hard day and complain to you about it." She shrugs. "All I'm asking you to do right now is listen and let me know what you hear."

"You're asking me to be an informant against a crime family, if what you're saying is true about them. That sounds extremely dangerous." My heart starts racing with trepidation at the very thought of betraying Gabriel like that. His uncle Peter was an informant for the FBI and put Gabriel's father in jail.

His uncle now has a hit man after him, courtesy of Gabriel's father.

What would the family do if they found out I was working with her?

Her lips twist, but she doesn't deny it. "I'll bet you'd like to have your father's sentence reduced."

And there it is. The carrot the FBI will dangle to try to lure me in. I'm so goddamn sick of people dangling my father in front of me like bait.

"I don't want his sentence reduced. I want him *out* of prison. He doesn't belong in there." She just admitted as much.

Kennedy frowns in thought. "Depending on what you bring to me, that could be arranged. That, and a new life for the both of you, so you're safe from harm."

Is she telling the truth?

If the FBI could arrange for my father's release... I wouldn't need Justin DeHavilland and that enormous bank account of drug money to pay his fees. I wouldn't have to wait months—possibly years—for the court system to work in our favor.

I wouldn't need Gabriel at all.

A sound carries in the hallway, pulling Kennedy's attention to the door. She slides a business card out of her robe pocket. I watch her stroll over and slip it into the robe I hung on the hook by the door. "Think about my offer, Mercy. It's a good one. You'll be helping *a lot* of people." She reaches for the handle, but then hesitates. "Oh, and I would suggest you *not* mention this conversation to Gabriel, especially if you happen to know more than you're letting on. *Especially* if you know anything that could be used against him in court. Witnesses against the Easton family have a habit of vanishing. Gabriel's a dangerous man. Don't be fooled by his charm." She ducks out, leaving me tense and stewing in my thoughts.

Do I know anything that could be used against Gabriel or Caleb in court? I don't think so. At least, not as key witness testimony. Nothing they could build an entire case on. Well, unless their case was about the illegal prison fight ring the brothers run. Gabriel outright admitted it to me. Would my word be considered solid evidence?

In any case, it doesn't sound like the FBI is after them for that. They want to take down the "family business," the one Gabriel's father and uncle are now dueling over. The one Gabriel doesn't want. He's trying to get away from it. He was born into it. It's his father that's the real problem. And this Uncle Peter, who's trying to kill him. What if I could help bury that guy while protecting Gabriel?

I lie trapped on the table, weighing Kennedy's offer, knowing Gabriel would never forgive me for working with her. Would he go as far as to send one of his goons after me? I don't want to find out.

The door creaks open again, and this time Anna enters. "Oh! Your eye mask slipped off."

"Uh... yeah."

She mock pouts. "How are you feeling, otherwise?"

Like I want to leave this spa and run far, far away.

SIX
GABRIEL

"Not even a good ol' fashioned plane bombing can keep you two down. Impressive." Vince Perri strolls off the elevator and into the penthouse with his hands in his pockets and a smirk on his face, as if he owns this place and we're just visitors here. His younger brother, Merrick, is on his heels, looking less casual. His poker face would sink him in two rounds.

"Well, that's us, isn't it? *Impressive*." Caleb is composed as he pours a round of vodka with surprising accuracy for having only one fully operational eye. He slides the glasses across the bar with the tip of his index finger. I know his composure is an act. He's still not a hundred percent convinced that the Perris weren't behind last night's explosion, even though our father has all but confirmed it was Uncle Peter. But my gut tells me these two had nothing to do with it, and I've learned to always trust my gut. Besides, they wouldn't be walking had Camillo or Miles Perri discovered our secret arrangement, and from what I can see, they don't even have a scratch to suggest that.

But when Caleb is suspicious, the tension that swirls around him is thick enough to choke a herd of elephants.

Merrick spares Farley—standing sentry in the corner but ready to pounce, quick as a panther; the behemoth is surprisingly sprightly—nothing more than a glance before closing the distance to the bar and accepting a drink. "Still think we tried to kill you?" he asks with equal calm, his eyes steady on Caleb's battered face. But his free hand is flexing by his thigh, looking ready to either ball up or reach for his gun at any indication of a trap.

Besides our loaded Glocks, Farley is our only protection in the room. He's the one we trust unequivocally. If we tell him to dig a hole, he'll ask how deep and nothing else. He's like our Bane, only not a psychopath.

The other security detail is watching the entryways into the hotel and the elevator, except for Moe, who was instructed to stay glued to Mercy. Caleb argued with me for the last hour about having the Perris stripped of their weapons before being allowed up here. I argued against it. We're supposed to be partners, not adversaries trying to kill each other at every turn. Plus, if I were these two, the hell if I would step foot inside this room unarmed, knowing we suspected them of attempted murder for even a second.

Now I'm wondering if *I'm* the idiot. Vince may be the convict with a history for violent assault, but Merrick is the highly trained MMA fighter. While Caleb and I can hold our own, we're no match for the youngest Perri, guns or not.

"We know it was Peter," I jump in to say before my cocky brother makes the tension worse.

"It *is* his MO." Vince accepts his drink and, though he put on a façade of calm, his shoulders seem to drop through his sip, as if he's finally allowed himself a breath. "He actually admitted to it?" His eyes flicker to Caleb's battered face, and I see the question there—has the threat been neutralized? Did we spend our night watching as Farley dug a hole in the desert?

Has Nonna Perri finally been avenged?

A part of me wishes I could say yes. "No, not exactly. But they've gone to ground. All of them. Peter, Vic, Alexei—"

"Hiding like the bunch of fucking rats they are," Caleb growls, downing a gulp only to wince. The vodka must be burning into that nasty cut.

Merrick steals a look at his brother. "This is a problem."

"No, it's not. It might change things, but the end result is the same. And if Peter's willing to try to take us out, then you can bet your ass he's after our father, too." There's a strong possibility that the Easton patriarchs will take each other out and our hands stay clean. Relatively so.

"In fact, we don't really need you two, do we?" Caleb smirks, though there's no humor in his words.

He's right. Who thought Uncle Peter would have the balls to come after us like this? He should have done it years ago instead of going all turncoat. Then again, he needed us. We're a hell of a lot smarter than his idiot sons. We launder quadruple what all their businesses combined can manage.

But now that he's been outed as an informant, the clock is ticking. He knows it's either him or us.

Another fleeting look passes between the two Perri brothers. They've figured out the same.

"So, what are you saying?" Vince asks, his face stony. "What the fuck are we even doing here?"

"Don't get your panties in a knot, Perri. Like Gabe said, the end result is the same. We just have to play our cards right." Caleb flips the channels on the TV from soccer to golf, as if we're in the middle of a casual conversation.

"Miles is going to get exactly what he deserves for what he did to our mother."

"Only if you deal with your uncle before he gets to you," Merrick mutters.

"We will. We've got people turning over rocks." I don't give a shit what our father said about taking care of the Peter problem himself. We need to know where he is and *now* for our plan to work. Having both Bane and our PI, Stan, on the hunt will net faster results.

"And what about those fuckhead cousins of yours?" Merrick asks.

Caleb lights a cigarette. "What about them?"

"We didn't expect them to go on the offensive, is all. Are we going to have to watch over our shoulders for the next thirty years?"

A haze of smoke curls from Caleb's lips as he levels Merrick with a steady gaze. "What's the matter? Are your little Perri feet getting cold?"

"Fuck you," Merrick sneers.

He grins in answer. "Our cousins are as good as dead. Bane's after them, too."

The brothers share a glance.

"Well, in that case..." Vince holds his glass up in a toast. "To finally being free of our families."

"Don't get ahead of yourself. A lot can go wrong before anything goes right," Caleb, ever the pessimist, warns, though he clinks his glass all the same.

"Until then..." Vince's astute crystal blue gaze wanders over the palatial suite, his posture visibly relaxing, his hands no longer looking ready to go on the attack "Have to say, this isn't how I expected the Easton boys to do Vegas."

Caleb snorts. "What'd you expect? A baby and a tiger?"

"More like a room full of booze and pussy to greet us."

"Booze is already here. The pussy will arrive later, but it's all for us. You'll need to find your own entertainment tonight." Caleb smirks through a sip. "If you're nice to me, I might let you watch. *This* is what you're really after anyway, isn't it?" His steely gaze lands on Merrick as he cups his crotch.

Fucking hell, Caleb. The guy's boyfriend was murdered by his own brother a month ago, and Caleb's throwing around "come get my dick" jokes already?

The glower that overtakes Merrick's face proves he doesn't find the taunt amusing either.

Farley takes a looming step closer, and I take two quick ones, to create a barrier and to squash the impending eruption. "Are we set for tonight?"

Vince shakes his head at Caleb before turning back to me. He nods. "Ten o'clock sharp. They'll use the service elevator, to avoid the Feds. You know the Feds are camped out downstairs, right?"

Caleb snorts, as if the idea that we wouldn't know is preposterous. After last night's fiasco, we assumed we'd earn one sooner or later. Moe is the one who noticed the unmarked gray van tailing us on the interstate. "Of course we know, and they can suck my dick because they don't have shit on us."

We *hope* they don't.Ten tonight is perfect. Our concierge, a petite blond named Daniela who Caleb is already sizing up for a blow job, made reservations for us at the Mage's high-end restaurant for seven, followed by VIP tickets to the circus show for the ladies. I don't give a fuck about watching a bunch of dudes in tights swing around on ropes, but Michelle said Mercy has always wanted to go, so I made sure to get the full experience—prime seats, a meet and greet with the cast after, the whole shebang. It'll keep them far away from here while Camillo and Miles are around.

Part of me wants to postpone this dog-and-pony show until tomorrow. It's all a pointless charade, a means to making it look like we're good sons following directives from the powers that be: my father. It's better to just get it over with though. A quick in-and-out meet-up and then I can enjoy the rest of this trip, ideally buried between Mercy's thighs.

I nod even as my stomach clenches at the prospect of inviting those snakes in here. The games room in our suite is the most secure location we'll find anywhere in Vegas. Farley has thoroughly swept the place for bugs.

But with all the bad blood between our two families and the fact that Miles is a sick fuck, even without the older generation Eastons there, things could go sideways and fast. All it'll take is one side comment about our mother, and my volatile brother's liable to start sinking bullet holes into the walls, and then the Feds *will* have shit on us.

Do we have a hope in hell of pulling this off?

We have to if we want a chance at a legitimate life.

With that in mind, I set my jaw with determination. "You two know your family better than we do. Let's play out a few scenarios on how they're going to want to handle the cartel situation, so we keep up appearances of this alliance—"

"Excuse me, Gabe, but the ladies are on their way back," Farley suddenly interrupts, his baritone voice a deep rumble cutting into our conversation.

"What do you mean, they're coming back?" I glance at my watch. We sent them away for four hours to give us time to work through details about tonight. It hasn't even been two.

"They're already in the elevator." Farley taps his ear where an earpiece sits. "They'll be here momentarily."

Shit. I didn't want Mercy knowing that we were meeting with the Perris again. She knows too much as it is. The first gathering with them at Empire ended in a fight and her snooping around in old newspaper articles, digging up dirt that could—should—have sent her running, our deal be damned. She's put pieces together to figure out that Camillo was responsible for our mother's death. Now she'll start worrying about me doing something stupid and dangerous. As much as I find I like her worrying about me, I don't want her *anywhere* near this.

What would Mercy even say if she found out we were masterminding a series of murders? Would she see it for what it is—a necessary means to an end?—or would she write me off as the devil that our father has worked so hard to raise me to be? There was a time when her opinion of me didn't matter, when she was a sexual conquest and nothing more.

But now I'm finding that I care what I see reflecting back when I look into her beautiful brown eyes. I don't want her to ever stop looking at me the way she does.

Caleb shakes his head and spears me with a told-you-so look. He insisted that bringing them would complicate things. He was all for leaving them in Phoenix with Moe. *I'm* the one who dug my heels in about bringing Mercy, because I'm a selfish ass who wants her nearby, who doesn't want to go a night without waking up next to her. "Let's move this conversation into the private room, shall we?" He grabs the closest bottle of booze.

I sigh, pulling my wallet out to see how much cash I have. I'd rather send them out to shop than have them sit here wondering what's going on behind closed doors. "Give me a few minutes to clear them out—"

The elevator doors open, and Mercy steps out, her face chalky-white, looking ready to spill her guts all over the cool tile entryway.

SEVEN
MERCY

I CONCENTRATE on my breathing as the elevator climbs the levels, praying I don't pass out before we reach the top. The *last* thing I want is Moe's hands on my body as he peels me off the floor.

"Do you think it might have been that chicken sandwich?" Michelle's voice is full of worry as she studies my face, which must be as white as death given how nauseous I feel. I wonder if the sheen of cold sweat I feel building on my forehead is visible.

"Yeah. Maybe." I force a weak smile as I lie to my best friend. What choice do I have, especially with Moe hovering?

As the esthetician unraveled my body from the plastic wrap, I dwelled on Agent Lewis—on all she already knows about me, on her offer, and her warning. I imagined my father getting away from that hellhole and starting over fresh. I combed through every sordid detail I know about Gabriel—what I can confirm and what I can deduce. I already know too much. I could know a lot *more*, given enough time.

Then I replayed our conversation from early today, coiled around each other's bodies with the sun cresting over the horizon, where he basically said that working with the Feds against his family would earn anyone a death sentence, blood relation or not.

By the time I made my way to the shower to rinse off the layer of chocolate on my skin, I'd convinced myself that my days of breathing are numbered.

So I bolted for my robe, canceling the rest of my session as my stomach churned and my lungs worked overtime to pull in air. I intended on leaving a message for Michelle to stay and enjoy the afternoon, but we crossed paths in the hallway, and after one look at my face, she insisted on escorting me back. I didn't have the energy to argue with her then. Now, I'm happy I didn't. If I had, I might be forced to cling to Moe instead.

"We're almost there," she says, smoothing her hand over my forearm comfortingly. "I'm so sorry."

"Why? It's not your fault," I mutter.

Moe stands silent behind us, having said nothing beyond a quick directive into his earpiece to let the others know were coming back. But I feel his sharp gaze boring into my skull, studying me, and it only escalates my panic. Does he suspect this is more than the effects of a bad sandwich? Could he have seen Agent Lewis in the spa and identified her for what she is? Gabriel said he was highly trained. Does that include sniffing out FBI agents?

How did the Feds even know I was going to be at the spa? And how did they know we would end up in Vegas today, after last night's tragedy? Have they been tailing us? Do they have Gabriel or Caleb bugged? Is someone informing on the Easton family? I shouldn't be surprised that the FBI are actively investigating them, but does Gabriel know?

I have so many questions, and I don't know if I can ask *any* of them.

The elevator doors slide open with a soft ding. The first face I see is Gabriel's, and it brings me an unexpected wave of relief. I release a lung's worth of air as I step out.

That relief is erased in the next breath as I spot Caleb by the bar with two familiar-looking men. It takes me only a moment to recognize them as the two guys they met with at Empire last week.

The Perris.

I know who they are. Or rather, who their father is—the man responsible for their mother's brutal death. What the hell are Gabriel and Caleb doing meeting with them again? Is this a friendly visit, or are they the reason we came to Vegas in the first place?

I don't have time to ponder that before Gabriel charges for me.

"What happened?" Concern mars his handsome face.

I swallow, struggling to find words as I feel all eyes on me. The weight of Agent Lewis's business card in my purse is noticeable. Could I explain myself if they found me with it? Would they believe me if I said I'm not working with FBI, that I haven't given them anything?

I should have torn that stupid piece of paper to shreds and left it in the spa trash can, is what I should have done. If not for my father, I would have.

When I don't answer, Gabriel shifts his gaze to Moe and barks, "What the fuck happened down there? You were supposed to watch her!"

"It must have been the sandwich or something. I don't know," I mumble.

Gabriel's eyes snap back to me. "You're sick?" His tone has softened instantly.

"I'll be fine. I just need to lie down for a bit until this passes."

"Come on." He slips an arm around my waist and deftly scoops me off the ground. I find myself sinking against his chest, comforted by his strength and the smell of his spicy cologne and the concern he's showing as he swiftly carries me past the men without a single word to them, up the stairs, and into our bedroom suite.

"Here." He rips the covers off the bed and sets me down gently. "What do you need? Water? Medicine? Should I call a doctor?"

"No doctor." They can't help me, aside from dosing me with Valium to dull this overwhelming dread that has taken hold of me.

"Wait here." He strolls into the en suite. I hug myself and listen as the sink faucet runs. When he returns, he has a folded white facecloth in hand and he's snagged the bottle of Evian from the table.

A knock on the door sounds, and a moment later it cracks open. I'm expecting Michelle, but instead Caleb pokes his head in. "Here." He thrusts an ice bucket into Gabe's hand. "In case she yackity-yacks."

I grimace. "I'll bet the staff would love that."

Gabriel pushes the door shut, locking it this time. "They'd love it more than cleaning puke up off the carpet if you can't make it in time."

"Fair enough."

He settles down on the edge of the mattress. "Besides, I'm sure it's not the worst thing they've had to clean up." He brushes strands of hair off my face with soft fingertips and then settles the damp towel against my forehead. Consternation shines in his eyes. "Does that help?"

"Yeah." As does being near Gabriel, oddly enough, especially when he dotes on me like this. Like a loving partner. Not like the dangerous criminal Agent Lewis claims him to be.

He has a handgun tucked in the back of his pants, I remind myself. And one in an ankle holster. And I just interrupted a meeting with a rival crime family. *The* rival crime family that is behind his mother's murder.

Still…

Minutes pass in silence as Gabriel rubs my nape with cool fingers and I study his hard jaw and those full lips that are capable of such softness. Maybe I should tell him about Agent Lewis's surprise visit. I didn't do anything wrong, and I told her nothing. He'd want to know that they're investigating him so he could take necessary precautions, to make sure he doesn't end up behind bars right when he's trying to break free of it all.

"Feeling better?"

I manage a weak smile. "A bit."

He nods. "I'll have the concierge rebook for tomorrow." His warm palm smooths back and forth over my thigh in loving strokes. "Your skin feels like silk."

"I got a chocolate body wrap."

"A chocolate body wrap," he echoes, inhaling. "So that's what I smell." His hand pushes the hem of my skirt up. "Do you taste like chocolate, too?"

Longing stirs in my lower belly, despite everything. "I don't know. I might taste like oil and body cream."

"That doesn't sound so bad, either." His gaze is searing as it drags over my bare legs, as he pushes my skirt even higher, revealing the lace of my panties. I know that look.

He's pondering the idea of pushing my thighs apart and finding out what my skin tastes like. In this short sundress, it wouldn't take much work on his part. With my frazzled nerves, I think it'd be a welcomed distraction.

But then he sighs heavily, his attention veering to the door. A soft curse slips from his lips.

"You have somewhere you need to be?"

"I shouldn't leave Caleb alone with them. He's liable to say something fucking stupid and tear this whole deal to shreds."

"The *hotel* deal?" I ask before I can stop myself.

He hesitates a moment before shaking his head.

The "family" business, then.

Their drug enterprise.

"You're going into business with *them*?" I can't help the accusation in my tone. "What happened to going legit?" Was he lying to me? Am I a fool to believe that will ever happen?

"We're *not* going into business with the Perris." A dark chuckle escapes his lips, as if the idea is absurd. "It's just.... It's complicated."

"Complicated how?"

His gaze drifts out past the wall of windows that overlooks the city. "Merrick and Vince are like us. They want out, too. But their father and older brothers are..." His brow pulls tights. "They're like my father."

"They want them to carry on the family business."

"Yeah."

"What is it with these old crime bosses being so desperate to breed more criminals?" I mutter, earning his chuckle.

"Anyway, we need their help to break free of my father's reach, and they need our help, too. So we're helping each other. That's all this is." He guides my skirt back down, flattening it with his palm.

I bite my tongue against the urge to ask how. The less I know, the better. That way I'll have nothing to tell the FBI and the Easton family won't label me a witness in need of extermination.

But what surprises me is how freely Gabriel is speaking to me about his family's business now. Granted, he's still guarded, but it's like a switch has been flipped with him lately, where he actually *wants* to divulge his secrets to me.

Like he trusts me.

Like he might get comfortable enough to complain about his day, to get "careless," as Agent Lewis suggested.

Maybe it's a residual of nearly dying together last night. Or maybe this is what happens when a guy like him falls in love. In any case, a few more weeks of this and there is a real possibility that Gabriel will divulge something that the FBI can use to bring down their entire dirty empire. Something that will earn my father's freedom from prison.

That prospect doesn't bring the wave of excitement and hope that I would have expected it to. Instead, a sharp pang of guilt stirs in my chest.

I swallow against the sickly feeling. "I'm sure I'm better off not knowing." My voice sounds off, shaky.

"You are." Gabriel stands. "Will you be up to dinner in a few hours?"

"I hope so. Why?"

"We have reservations for seven, and then you and Michelle are going to a show after." A small smile touches his lips. "She said you've been dying to see Cirque du Soleil, so I got you tickets. They're good ones."

"You won't be coming?" My voice is laced with disappointment.

"No, but don't worry, Moe will be with you."

"Fantastic," I mutter.

"Don't worry, he'll blend in. You won't even notice him."

"Like at the spa today?" The receptionist looked only too happy to wave goodbye to our backs.

Gabriel rubs his forehead. "I've got a lot on my mind right now. I'm not doing this again. Until we have a handle on my uncle, you're not leaving here without protection, and that's final."

Normally, I might be irritated with this domineering side of him, but for once I don't mind. In fact, if I go back there tomorrow, I'm going to ask Moe to stand outside my treatment door. "It's not him. Well, part of it is him."

"And what's the other part?"

I hesitate. "I just thought this trip was about us and I'm beginning to feel like an accessory." One that could be swapped out for any number of females. That bothers me far more than I'd like to admit.

"You're not an accessory, Mercy." He bites his bottom lip in thought. "I wish I could be at the show tonight."

I snort at the bold-faced lie. "Bullshit."

That earns me a smile. "I'd spend the whole time with my hand up your dress."

I feel his words between my thighs.

He sighs. "Caleb and I have something to take care of tonight and I don't want you around for it."

That sounds as ominous as last night's excursion. "It better not involve any women," I warn half-heartedly.

He winks. "Only a few."

I spear him with a glare that makes him laugh.

"No, there won't be *any* women at this meeting." He leans in to press a lingering kiss against my lips before whispering, "And there's only one woman for me. You know that."

My heart skips a beat before beginning to race. His candor with expressing his feelings of late has been a welcome change. "Do I?"

"You *should* by now." Our eyes are inches apart as he regards me, and I see a glimmer of vulnerability in them. "You fucking own me, Mercy." He presses his forehead to mine. "I never expected to feel about anyone like I do about you."

My hand moves of its own accord, reaching up to smooth over his chest, reveling in the plane of hard muscle before stalling over his heart. I think I'm beginning to see it. Why else would he go to all this effort and expense—twisted as it may be—to keep me around? Gabriel is surrounded by beautiful women. He could screw five different women every day. He probably did before I showed up.

For whatever reason, I've held his undivided attention long after he succeeded in his depraved conquest. I've seen him shift, soften. I've made him bend to my will, agreeing to things that seemed impossible. If I'm being honest with myself, having this kind of influence over Gabriel is addictive. Empowering.

But it's also not helping with this dreadful feeling in the pit of my stomach.

"Me neither," I manage to admit through a shaky voice. Never in a million years would I have expected to fall for this man, but he's taken up permanent residence in my thoughts.

He drops a kiss on the tip of my nose. "Get some rest. You've had a rough twenty-four hours."

I swallow the rising lump in my throat. "I'll try." Rest, and a chance to gather my conflicted thoughts.

I watch him round the bed, biting my tongue against the urge to ask him to forget everything and everyone else and curl up with me in bed. When he's around, nothing else matters. I don't think. Right now I desperately need to *not* think.

How much would it hurt him if I sold him out in exchange for my father?

And what happens when a man like Gabriel is hurt like that?

Betrayed like that.

He pauses at the door. "I can get you an Ambien, if you want." The corner of his mouth curls. "I wouldn't mind another show."

I feel my cheeks flush at his teasing. "I flushed my prescription after that night. Jerk."

"That's disappointing," he murmurs dryly and then ducks out, shutting the door softly behind him.

I feel his absence immediately.

I wait a few moments before I dare dig out Agent Lewis's business card from my purse, my impulsive fingers itching to rip up the card and keep playing the clueless girlfriend who sees nothing, knows nothing, says nothing. Who has her own reasons for getting enmeshed with a man like Gabriel Easton. That woman doesn't want Gabriel to go to jail. She doesn't want him punished. She wants him to detangle himself from his family mess and find an honest path forward.

With her.

Is that even possible, or is she a damn fool?

The practical side of me knows that I need to set aside my growing feelings for Gabriel, because where can things between us possibly go? I mean, he joked about eloping, and in two seconds I had a lengthy mental list of *all* the reasons he will never be marriage material. I'm only here in the first place because he's a reprobate who saw my weakness and exploited it.

I need to think about my father. Duncan Wheeler does not belong in prison.

Gabriel does.

And Justin DeHavilland may be the best of the best where pricey lawyers are concerned, but even he can't guarantee a successful appeal for my dad. What if all the money in the world can't give him his life back? What if Gabriel paying for his sins is the ticket to getting my father out?

What if I don't really have a choice here at all?

With growing dismay, I tug at a loose seam in my wallet, making the hole just large enough that I can fold the card and slip it in for safekeeping.

I PICK my way down the stairs to the main floor, acutely aware of Farley's observant gaze from his post by the elevator. I'd like to think it's concern for my safety, but the electric-blue silk dress and silver five-inch heels likely have more to do with the attention. Michelle stuffed half her closetful of dresses into her suitcase for this trip—all of them equally short and scandalous.

"They're waiting for you outside," Farley offers in a cartoonishly deep voice that I feel in the pit of my stomach.

I offer him a polite smile before strolling through the sliding doors into soft music over the speakers and Michelle's hysterical laughter by the lengthy outdoor bar. The dry August heat envelops me as I take in the expansive terrace and the hundred-and-eighty-degree view of the valley bathed in the setting sun.

Caleb notices me first while taking a long drag of a cigarette. I don't remember him smoking as much as he has been these last twenty-four hours. "Look who's returned to the land of the living." His hungry gaze is glued to my legs as I approach, and he's not bothering to hide it. I can only imagine the kinds of filthy thoughts going through that man's mind. He and his brother seem well in tune in that regard.

Michelle, looking decadent in a shimmering gold dress that I've never seen before, swivels her barstool to face me. She's beaming, whether because of the martini in her grasp or Caleb's fingers stroking her shoulder with affection, I can't be sure. "I *knew* that one would be perfect for you!"

"As long as I don't bend over."

"*Please* do." Caleb winks at me with his good eye. The swelling has gone down in the other one, leaving him with a more palatable, albeit ugly, bruised appearance.

"I went shopping. You like?" Michelle kicks her legs up to show off sparkly heels.

"Love." I ease onto a barstool. "Where's Gabriel?" He came to check on me about an hour ago. I hadn't slept a wink, my conscience spinning for hours, replaying the past weeks, hoping my heart could sink anchors into the ugly, depraved parts of him. But my mind just kept going back to his impish smile, the way our bodies move so well together, and how he's somehow slowed the downward spiral that had taken over my life, how I feel like I finally have an ounce of control again.

He ducked out without even attempting to climb on top of me, his thoughts seemingly occupied elsewhere. Likely on whatever he has cooking up with those Perri brothers.

"He had to grab something downstairs. He should be back soon. So?" Caleb leaves his spot tucked in beside Michelle to round the bar. He holds up a shaker and an empty martini glass. "How dirty do you want it?"

"Just a little dirty. And not too strong, please." I haven't eaten since this morning, and my appetite is nonexistent. I'm liable to be stumbling after my first sip.

"Really? I'm surprised." He reaches for the bottle of gin. "Gabriel said you like it *really* dirty."

My face flushes. "Does *everything* have to be a sexual suggestion with you?" At least he's back to his easygoing playboy self.

"Hey, I'm just trying to be a good guy and make you the best martini you've ever tasted," he says with mock innocence.

"Oh, oh, oh!" Michelle slaps the bar counter with excitement before tipping her glass back to polish off her drink. "Do your thing again!"

Caleb quirks a brow. "*My thing?*"

"Yes. *Your thing.*" She sets her glass out to be refilled.

"I don't know what *thing* you speak of." He flips a tumbler in the air, catching it deftly.

"Yes! That!" Michelle props her chin on her palm and regards Caleb with a drunken, dreamy gaze. "And you can make mine *extra* dirty this time."

"Extra?" he echoes, the beginnings of a sly smirk touching his lips.

"Yeah. The dirtiest you've ever made." Her eyes twinkle as she delivers that in a seductive voice.

You have no idea what you're in for, Michelle.

With a boyish chuckle that softens the chiseled edges of his face, Caleb sets out making us a round of martinis, glasses and shakers spinning this way and that with skillful precision.

"Someone's been practicing their Tom Cruise moves," I tease, though I'm impressed when he tosses the bottle of gin into the air and catches it by the neck. "How many of those have you broken?"

"Too many to count." Caleb reaches for the vermouth. "Gabe was so pissed when he figured out the insane breakage report was because of me and not the staff." He spins the bottle once before pouring a shot. "He only lets me play with the bar well shit."

I spy the shelf behind him that holds several bottles. I don't recognize the brand names. "The stuff you're playing with now isn't bar well."

"Come on, Mercy," he drawls. "You know me well enough by now."

"Unfortunately." The guy's favorite morning pastime is indecent exposure.

I know you won't handle prison well.

If the FBI is building a case against Gabriel, they're also targeting his brother and partner in crime, which means I wouldn't just be betraying Gabriel by working with them.

A fresh wave of dread swirls in my stomach. Tucked away neatly beneath Caleb's playboy charm is a man with a scalding temper. I've only seen glimpses of it—that night at Empire before they met with Merrick and Vince Perri; last night, as he was downing scotch and loading guns.

What lengths would Caleb go to protect not only himself but his brother?

What is he capable of?

My eyes graze the handgun set on the edge of the bar. At least the safety's on—my father taught me enough that I can identify the indicator—but it's within easy reach.

I'm so deep in thought that I don't notice anyone approaching until a hand glides against my bare back, startling me enough that I jump.

"*Easy*," Gabriel purrs, pulling me backward into his body.

I close my eyes and try to relax as he slips his arm around my waist, flattening his palm against my belly.

"You still smell like chocolate." He leans in to press hot lips against my neck. "You're up for dinner?"

Eating is the absolute last thing I can think of right now. "Something small, maybe?"

"Whatever you feel like, babe." Fingers hook my chin, guiding my face to his. "You look beautiful tonight." Gabriel seems unfazed by our audience as his mouth captures mine in a slow, seductive kiss, his tongue slipping along the seam of my lips in a teasing stroke. It stirs an instant ache in my body, and I feel myself melting into his chest, wanting to skip dinner and the show and hid in the bedroom with him for the rest of our trip.

"Two martinis for the ladies. One lame missionary style"—Caleb sets a glass in front of me and then slides one toward Michelle, complete with three fat green olives on a spike—"and one so dirty, you'll still feel it in the morning."

"Promises, promises." Michelle makes a provocative show of popping all three olives into her mouth, earning Caleb's groan and playful knuckle-bite.

I distract myself from this little act of foreplay with a sip of my drink, turning my undivided attention back to Gabriel. "So, what have you been up to?"

"This and that," he answers evasively.

"That doesn't sound suspicious at all." What time did their "guests" leave?

He slips his hand into his pocket to pull out a small

square black velvet box with Michelle's family jewelry store insignia and holds it out for me.

My stomach drops. "*What is that?*" Sharp accusation cuts into my tone. It looks a hell of a lot like a ring box. I glare at Michelle, who can't contain her knowing grin. She's in on this.

Gabriel chuckles. "*Relax*, Mercy. It's just a graduation gift."

"Damn, bro. I don't think she has high hopes for you two." Caleb sets a tumbler of something amber on the counter in front of Gabriel.

"Yeah, I'm starting to get that vibe. Should I be worried?"

"Open it!" Michelle demands, still giddy.

With a mixture of apprehension and excitement, I crack open the lid. My jaw drops.

"I remembered you noticing it when you came into the store last," she says by way of explanation.

"Well, *yeah*." *Of course* I noticed it. The price tag on the stunning diamond paloma ring was mind-blowing. I couldn't fathom anyone having that kind of disposable income. Her dad keeps a decoy of it in a special glass case in the wall. The real one, he keeps in the vault.

Kept in the vault.

Gabriel collects the piece from its secure resting spot and deftly slips it onto the middle finger of my left hand. "It fits perfectly."

"I can't accept this," I begin to say, stumbling over my words as I stretch my hand in front of me to regard the countless diamonds. It's more beautiful than I imagined.

"Yeah, you can." Gabriel's lips tickle my jawline. "Just don't wear it to visit your father."

"Are you kidding me? I'll be terrified to wear it *anywhere*."

"So I guess we're doing gifts now then?" Caleb pulls his phone out of his pocket, clicks a few buttons and then unceremoniously drops it on the counter beside my drink. "Congrats. Pick your color."

My confused gaze flips from the sleek sports car staring up at me to him back to the page. "What are you talking about?"

"What do you want? Black? White? Silver? I figured you'd want to choose, but I can go ahead and order it if you don't care. Blue suits you."

His intentions finally register. "You can't buy me a *car*!"

"Do you remember chewing my ass out for hauling your shitbox away?"

"Yes, but—"

"I owe you a new car, so I'm buying you a new car. Simple." His brow furrows with annoyance.

He *did* have my car towed to the scrapyard without asking. "I had a Toyota Camry."

Caleb snorts. "Yeah, you're not parking a fucking Camry in our driveway. We Eastons have standards. Have you not noticed?" He waves a hand around the terrace.

I laugh at the absurdity of this conversation. "And I can't park a Mercedes outside my apartment. It'll get jacked by morning."

"*Your apartment?*" Caleb shakes his head, his amused attention shifting to Gabriel. "She hasn't figured it out yet, has she?"

"She's stubborn." Gabriel scans his watch. "Shit, I need you to come with me." He collects my drink and, taking my hand, guides me off my stool and leads me over to one of two expansive sectionals sheltered beneath the enormous roof overhang. An iPad sits propped open on the coffee table. "Use these." He digs a set of AirPods from his pocket.

"What's going on?" I ask, tucking the earpieces into my ears without much thought, my head still in a fog thanks to the barrage of outrageous gifts.

"Just something that might make you feel a bit better."

Almost immediately, the iPad chimes with an incoming video call from an unknown number.

"Someone's calling—"

"You've got fifteen minutes. And if he tells anyone, these perks will vanish." Gabriel hits the Accept button and ducks out of the frame just before my father appears on the screen.

"Dad?" As much as I hate seeing him in that orange jumpsuit, warmth spreads through my chest at his surprised face. I'm guessing it mirrors mine.

"You got about as much warning as I did, then," he says, chuckling softly.

I break my gaze free from the screen long enough to locate Gabriel, strolling backward toward the glass doors, watching me. Arranging this must have cost him a lot. Not as much as the visit to the infirmary, but *still*. The ring was an extravagant gift. *This*? This is worth a thousand diamond rings to me. That he went to the effort...

"Thank you," I mouth, my throat clogging up with emotion. He needs to stop doing sweet, thoughtful things like this.

A satisfied smile stretches across his face as he disappears inside.

"That one guard... Danny or Donny... something like that... he pulled me out of my cell. Wouldn't tell me anything. I thought I was getting walked into something I might not walk out of. Almost pissed my pants. Anyway, he led me down here into *this* room." Dad frowns as he searches the barren gray walls. "This was all set up already. I just had to hit the call button."

"Justin DeHavilland," I hear myself lie. "He pulled some strings."

"Oh yeah?" Dad worries his lip. The bruises and scrapes that marred his face the last time I saw him are healing nicely. A few more weeks and all physical evidence that he was nearly killed will have faded. "And what about on your end, then? Who set you up over there?"

My dad's no idiot. He's already plenty suspicious of recent events—the high-priced lawyer suddenly swooping in, the guards giving him a wide berth, the way his attacker died in solitary. I can't blame him. I also can't tell him the truth.

"A friend."

"A friend." His eyes narrow. "Mercy—"

"We only have fifteen minutes to talk, Dad."

"And I want to spend those minutes making sure you aren't doing something stupid on my account."

I'm doing plenty of stupid things on your account. "Please? Now's not the time for the third degree. What matters is that we're talking, right?"

That stalls his tongue. A moment later, he nods. "Speaking of degrees... how'd your exams go?"

A wide, genuine smile stretches across my face. "I'm finished!" The reality of that hasn't sunk in, sufficiently thwarted by everything else.

"And you think you passed? You're plenty smart enough to," he adds quickly. "I just know you were worried for a while there, with all my shit going on to distract you."

"I'm good. I studied my ass off."

"Well, then...." His shoulders sag with a relieved sigh. "Good for you. I'm so proud of you, girl."

I freeze my happy expression. He wouldn't be proud of me if he knew about my arrangement with Gabriel.

"You look great, by the way."

"Thank you."

Michelle bursts out in laughter at something Caleb says, and my father's eyes light up. "I recognize that laugh. Tell her I said hi." His eyes flitter around the screen, taking in my surroundings, frowning curiously. "So, where are you now? Looks like somewhere fancy."

"Vegas, for a few days." I hesitate. "We're celebrating." While my father rots in a cell. That ever-familiar pang of guilt stirs.

"A night on the town." He nods with approval. "Good for you, Mercy. You're finally getting out there and living your life again. I can't tell you how happy I am to hear that."

"You'll get to do that again too, Dad."

The smile that answers is sad. "Honey, I don't think you should pin all your hopes on this fancy lawyer—"

"He's already working on your appeal. You *will* get out of there," I say with as much conviction in my voice as possible. I have to believe it. "One way or another. I will do *whatever* I have to, to get you out of there."

He shakes his head. "You see, that's what I'm worried about, Mercy. Listen to me carefully. I don't know what you've done up until now, but I need you to *promise* me you're not putting yourself in danger. If *anything* ever happened to you because of me, I wouldn't be able to live with myself. I'll wish Diego had finished me off."

"Don't say that—"

"*Promise* me, Mercy." His voice has grown husky as he stares me down through the screen.

I avert my gaze, gathering the courage to lie to him. That's when I notice the motionless figure slouched in a lounge chair in the corner of the terrace maybe ten feet away from me, his muscular arms folded across his chest, his legs splayed, mirrored sunglasses shielding those cunning eyes from view. By all appearances, Moe is catching sleep, and yet I have this eerie feeling that he's watching me.

I hadn't noticed him there earlier, but he could have arrived with Gabriel. Or, as Gabriel claims, he's an expert at blending into his surroundings. Even asleep, I'm betting he'd be on his feet, gun in hand, at the slightest hint of a threat. All these guys are probably the same.

"I'm safe, Dad. As safe as I ever have been, anyway. Maybe safer." It's a lie, but the moment I say it out loud, I also know it to be true. The reality is, I've never truly been safe. My childhood was spent around a heroin addict. Near the end, Mom was known to disappear for weeks at a time, leaving my father and me to fend for ourselves. My father is in prison because I was attacked by his coworker. I live in a run-down apartment building frequented by police. There are no white picket fences and neighborly muffin drops in my life.

And, sure, the events of last night are directly linked to being with Gabriel, but at least now I'm surrounded by highly trained bodyguards and a man who isn't taking chances with my safety.

Dad hesitates. "And you're not caught up with anyone you don't want to be with?"

"No, Dad. I'm *good*." That much is true.

His tired eyes bore into me for another long moment before he finally sighs reluctantly. He looks exhausted.

"Just make sure you don't tell anyone about this, okay?"

He waves my warning off. "I see how these things work

around here. Someone's pockets sure are getting fat on my account."

"Things are good, though?"

"You could say that." His gaze wanders around the room they stuck him in. "I've been eating lunch with this guy lately. They call him Chops and, boy, is he one mean-looking son of a bitch. Hands like bears paws, tattoos all over his skull, silver teeth. Anyway, he just came and sat down next to me one day and started eating, not talking. He did ask me for my chocolate pudding." He snorts. "At least he *asked*. Anyway, he came back the next day and the next. Crazy Bob said there's a prison fighting ring and he's the one to beat. Nobody messes with him."

That must be the beast I saw Gabriel meeting with the one time. "Glad you're making friends." Is Gabriel paying for that, too?

Dad chuckles, but then his expression smooths over to seriousness. "Tell *whoever* it is that's.... Well, you tell him thank you." Those words are dripping with reluctance. "You know, for this and for that visit to the infirmary. And for keeping me alive in here. I'm guessing I wouldn't be if it weren't for him."

Fuck. So Dad's figured out there's a specific "him" involved. Has he also figured out that this person isn't helping simply out of the goodness of his heart or for my delightful company?

Mixed in with my shame is the urge to defend Gabriel, to tell Dad that whatever he's imagining, it's not that bad. In fact, it's become mostly good. I'm here now because I want to be.

But my father will never accept Gabriel, no matter how many visits and calls he arranges, no matter who he lines up to watch my father's back.

I nod, even as my mind swirls.

Dad's right. He'd likely be dead by now if not for Gabriel. Twisted motives or not, Gabriel is the only reason my father will survive this. He's the only one willing to help me. Not the FBI or the police or the prison system. Agent Lewis knows my father doesn't belong in Fulcort on a murder conviction, but she isn't about to do anything about it. Not unless I risk my life to make her case.

"And don't worry, I won't say a word to anyone," Dad reiterates. "Not even Crazy Bob."

"How is your cellmate, anyway?" I ask, needing to move the conversation away from Gabriel Easton.

Dad shrugs. "Oh, you know. Still crazy."

"When did it happen?... *All of it?...* " Gabriel paces around the pool table, his hand shoved through his mane of brown hair, sending it into disarray. "Has Puff heard yet?"

Puff? Is that a person?

His feet stall when he notices me standing in the doorway of the games room, but after a moment he continues his pacing, answering whoever is on the other side of that phone with a series of grunts, his scowl growing more menacing. He's bothered by whatever he's been told, that much is obvious.

He ends the call abruptly and spins to face me. "What do you need?" His tone is sharp.

"I... I wanted to thank you for arranging the FaceTime with my father," I stammer, caught off guard. The sweet, playful mood he was in earlier when he slid this diamond ring on my finger is nowhere to be seen, replaced by this brooding man.

He sighs heavily and rubs a hand over his forehead as if to try to relief tension. "I'm sorry. I didn't mean to snap at you. I'm just stressed."

I pull the pocket doors closed behind me, shutting us into the long, narrow room. There is a modern cigar lounge vibe in here, with matte black walls and black marble tile floors. A bar with red leather stools fill one end. Behind it, a sizeable flatscreen TV fills the wall. An enormous and pristinely kept billiard table is next to the bar. Beside that is a massive poker table.

Even though I know I shouldn't—not when I'm in this state of confusion over what to do about Agent Lewis's offer —I find myself asking, "Do you want to talk about it?" Not because I'm digging for dirt to use as leverage. I genuinely want to lend him an ear. I find myself craving his conversation as much his physical affection, no matter how dark of a path those conversations often take.

He shakes his head. "I just got some bad news that will anger my father."

"Is it to do with your uncle?"

"No. It's about the family business." His lips twist in thought. When he speaks again, he seems to be choosing his words carefully. "Certain organizations are making a play for our territory. Caleb and I don't give a shit if they take it, but my father will, and this latest attack will set him off when he hears about it."

Attack? Is that just a figure of speech? "I guess it's a good thing he's in prison, then."

Gabriel's responding laughter is wicked. "That won't stop him. He can still make our lives hell, especially if he thinks we're not doing as he's asked. That's why we have this meeting tonight with the Perris."

The Perris? "Didn't you already meet with them this afternoon?" I ask warily.

"That was just Merrick and Vince. That was nothing. But now we have to get into a room with fucking Camillo and Miles Perri. Because it's what *he* wants. *I* don't want it. *I* think it's a really fucking bad idea. I don't trust them," he rants, the muscle in his jaw ticking. "That's why you can't be here tonight. I don't want those two knowing you exist. I sure as hell don't want them knowing how much you mean to me."

Holy shit. Camillo Perri. That's the man who killed their mother and got away with it. He's coming *here*? I don't blame Gabriel for his agitation. It's becoming clear that his father steers a lot of their choices, even from within his cage. "I'm sorry," I offer with genuine concern. "I wish I could make it better for you." After all he's done for me.

He leans against the poker table, folding his arms across his chest. "Did you have a good conversation with your father?"

"Yeah." I smile. "He said thanks."

Gabriel's eyebrows arch.

"I didn't tell him anything," I assure him, wandering around to the other side of the poker table, to where he stands. I smooth my palms over the silky soft material of his black dress shirt. It's meant to be a soothing gesture, but it allows me a chance to admire the curves of his hard chest, and trace his collarbone with my fingertips. "He figured out there's a man behind all of this protection, and he wanted to pass along a thank you for keeping him alive."

"He's welcome." Gabriel relaxes his stance and reaches up to stroke a wayward strand of hair off my forehead before his gaze searches my features. "He should know I would do *anything* for his daughter." The layer of frost that chilled his mood only moments ago seems to be thawing already.

I lean in to seal my lips over his in a teasing kiss, reveling in the heat that radiates from his body. "Did you also arrange for a scary prize fighter named Chops to eat lunch with him every day?"

"Prison rules, babe. It's all about who you sit with in there." Gabriel ropes his arms around my waist, pulling me flush against him. "He's okay with the company, right?"

"My dad gave him his chocolate pudding, so I'd say yes."

Gabriel chuckles. "Speaking of eating... " He checks his watch.

I groan, burrowing my face into his neck, inhaling his cologne. "Do we have to? Can't we stay here all night, like this? Just the two of us?" Because when I'm with him, I'm not doubting my judgement. I'm not hearing Agent Lewis's voice in my head.

He folds his arms around my shoulders, embracing me in warmth and comfort. "Wow. Who could have guessed that Mercy Wheeler would be *begging* to spend time with me?"

Not me. Not in a million years.

And yet here I am, slipping my hand between our bodies to palm his growing erection, teasing him, suddenly aching for a quick and dirty tryst, right here on this poker table.

He allows the casual stroking for a few moments, going as far as to reach beneath the hem of my dress and tug at my panties. But then he readjusts them and gives my ass an affectionate squeeze. "We should probably go."

"Wow. Who could have guessed that Gabriel Easton

would turn down an opportunity to get laid?" I echo his mocking tone, earning his chuckle.

"That's not it. It's just...." His throat bobs with a hard swallow as he studies me beneath a fringe of thick, dark lashes. "That's not the only reason I want you around."

My arched brow has him laughing harder. He cups my chin with two gentle hands, pulling my face into a tender kiss before whispering, "Come on. We have reservations, and my brother is a stickler for punctuality."

EIGHT
GABRIEL

"You sure you're finished?" The server stalls with his hand an inch away from Mercy's plate, frowning at her.

"Yes. Thanks." Mercy offers him a small smile. "The bit I had was delicious." She pats her belly as if to emphasize her claim.

It's a load of bullshit, and we all know it. She didn't eat *any* of her meal. She didn't even pretend to eat, didn't cut the chicken up into little pieces. She just pushed everything around on her plate so it doesn't look as pretty going back to the kitchen as it did coming out.

He collects the rest of the plates and takes off, but not before stealing a last glance at Mercy's tits. I can't blame him; I've been trying not to stare at them in that sexy blue dress all night. Better yet, they're all mine.

Eat your fucking heart out, asshole.

"You still feeling rough?"

"A bit," she admits, taking a large gulp of her drink, her eyes a touch glazed as she meets mine. She might not be eating, but she's definitely hitting those martinis hard.

"Well, you *look* good." She looks perfectly fine, nothing

like that pale ghost that stumbled off the elevator earlier. And yet I can't shake this feeling that something is off with her. She left for the spa all fired up, arguing with me about not needing Moe. But then she came back and curled up into a ball in bed. That's how I found her hours later, and since then she's been on edge, jumping when I touch her, tense beneath my fingers, sparing a few smiles and even fewer of her biting remarks that I love.

Granted, we were a minute away from being charred last night. The poor woman is probably still in shock.

Or does it have anything to do with me telling her how much she means to me? I've never been that open with a woman before. I've never cared like this about a woman before.

Did I scare her away with all that bullshit talk of feelings?

I can't believe I'm even worrying about this.

I ease my chair close enough that I can drape my arm over the back of hers and lean in to taste the skin on her neck, just below her ear. "I'll make sure you end the night feeling fantastic," I promise, smoothing my palm high up her thigh, fighting the urge to slip my fingers beneath this short dress to see if she's wet for me yet.

The responding tremble in her body sends blood racing straight to my groin.

"So, will you guys change everything or keep it the same but just change the name? Like, will this place stay like *this*?" Michelle's bright blue eyes flitter around our dimly lit alcove overlooking the city.

"Mr. Green" and "Mr. Pink Panther" were greeted at the hostess desk by Daniela, our concierge, and led here to what I'm assuming is the best table—one of many perks when you fork over the kind of coin we did to stay in that suite. Since then, two servers have tag-teamed us, making sure our drinks were never less than half full, our eyes never wandered for service, and our every need was catered to—and they managed to do it without being annoying. That's an impressive feat.

"Guess we'll have to see what the books look like. What's working and what's not." Caleb is radiating energy. He's excited about the prospect of owning this place.

"Don't go making too many plans," I warn. "We don't own shit yet. The current owner won't even talk to us. He might tell us to go fuck ourselves."

"Speak for yourself. Everyone loves me."

I snort. My brother's a pompous ass who pisses people off on the daily.

Our agent, Howard, gave us a full rundown of Bruce Cohen, the rich prick who owns a majority share of this place—a terrible businessman with a rampant drug problem who hasn't yet accepted the fact that the Mage is hemorrhaging money. So far, he's refused to take a meeting with Howard to discuss the idea of selling, which is kind of a big problem given we're here to meet with him. Word is, though, that Howard's not the only one breathing down his neck. We need to pinch this place at the right time, just before the bank takes it away from him and sells it to one of the big corporations that dominate the strip.

"We *will* meet with him before this trip is over." Caleb downs the rest of his drink. "And he's gonna sell to us. He's not going to have much choice."

Mercy gasps beside me, her eyes widening with horror.

It takes a second to dawn on me what she thinks my idiot brother meant. "Bankruptcy! The guy's running this place into the ground."

Her body sinks with a sigh of relief. "Oh."

"Jesus. Is that what you think of us?" That we're cold-blooded killers who cut down people just to get what we want? That thought bothers me more than it should.

Mercy cringes. "Sorry, I just.... Sorry." She weaves her fingers through the one I have settled on her thigh.

"Well, I think it's all *so* exciting." Michelle reaches over to squeeze Caleb's leg. "I better get a hotel room whenever I want."

With a Cheshire cat grin, Caleb curls his arm around Michelle's slender shoulder, pulling her to his side. "Babe, you'll always have a place *right here*." He guides her hand over his crotch.

She bellows with laughter, happily drowning in his attention.

I like her a lot. I like her with my brother. I'm guessing she won't like seeing him get his dick sucked by one of the show girls set to arrive later tonight after our little soiree with the Perris. What can I say, except my brother's my brother. I'm not a praying man, but if I was, I'd pray that she rolls with it and joins in. Otherwise, Mercy's going to have something else to be sour about.

"Excuse me," a voice interrupts. We turn to find the chef standing at our table, holding Mercy's dinner plate in his meaty hand. "May I ask what was wrong with your meal?" He glares at Mercy, his brow furrowed so deeply that his dumb chef hat starts sliding halfway down his forehead. Our server is standing five feet behind him, studying his shoes.

"Uh... nothing? It was lovely." Mercy stumbles over her words, likely as surprised to have the chef questioning her—and with a sharp tone—as I am. "I'm just getting over a stomach bug."

"If you're sick, then why order?" the chef presses, his

accent thick but unidentifiable. Mercy's cheeks are flushing as surrounding tables notice the exchange. "I could take it to go?"

"To go!" His face twists in horror. "It will be inedible! The pastry will be soggy!"

I'm biting my tongue, waiting for Mercy to unleash that acerbic attitude she's launched my way more than once, looking forward to it. But she simply stares with bewilderment in her eyes, as if she doesn't know what to make of this situation.

"Is this a fucking joke?" I finally snap.

"Maybe we're getting punked?" Caleb searches our surroundings.

"*Joke*? I *never* joke about my creations. And *this* is going straight into the dumpster now."

I exchange a what-the-fuck look with Caleb. "We're paying for your *creation* either way, so *relax*."

"*You people...*" The chef's mouth curls as if he's about to spit. "You're so wasteful."

"Yeah, yeah, it's the American way," Caleb mutters, quickly growing bored with the man. "You can go now, Wannabe Ramsay, and take your shitty creation with you."

The chef mutters something under his breath that I don't catch. What I do catch is the pointed sneer directed at Mercy.

I stand so fast, my chair topples over. Diners at surrounding tables turn in their seats at the commotion. They're about to get one hell of a show, one that will likely end in my arrest.

"How is everyone doing tonight!" A tiny bald man in a black suit storms in, waving his hands frantically. "I hope you enjoyed your meals? That's great!" He turns to the chef. "*Ralph,* it's time to go back to the kitchen now."

The chef glares at him with pure loathing.

"Now!" the man barks, pointing to the kitchen. It's almost comical, given Ralph is over six feet tall and easily tipping the scale over two hundred pounds. Meanwhile, this little man barely reaches his chest.

After another long, intense moment, Ralph spins on his heels and stalks off.

"Thanks for dinner, Ralph!" Caleb hollers loudly, waving at his back.

Ralph responds with a middle finger in the air, earning dropped jaws from Michelle and Mercy and a bark of laughter from Caleb. Meanwhile, my limbs are vibrating with rage. I'm trying to decide if I can spare Farley tonight to escort Ralph into the trunk of his car and out to a lonely desert road.

The man winces. "What can I say, he's passionate about his job."

"That asshole should not have a job," Caleb says. "If I owned this hotel, I'd fire him."

"I *do* own this hotel, and I've already been through three head chefs in the past six months," the man mutters, as if beaten down by that admission.

Caleb and I exchange glances. *This* is Bruce Cohen? The wild-child, coke-snorting, orgy-loving owner of the Mage who's dug his heels in on the reality of selling this place? He looks like Mr. Magoo.

"Allow me to cover your check as my apology for Ralph. And if there's anything else I can do—"

"Please. Take a load off and have a drink with us." Caleb makes an elaborate show of edging his chair over, capping it off with a victorious, shit-eating grin and a "told you so" wink at his brother.

NINE
MERCY

"Stop fidgeting!" Michelle scolds in a harsh whisper.

"I can't help it. I had too many drinks over dinner."

"Then use the restroom."

"Not *now*." We're only ten minutes into the first act. "I'm not fidgeting *that* bad."

She pries her mesmerized gaze from the stage of acrobats long enough to spare me an exasperated stare. "You're squirming worse than Bo. How can you enjoy the show?"

Fantastic. She's comparing me to her hyperactive two-year-old nephew. The truth is, I'm not enjoying the show and it has nothing to do with my full bladder. I haven't been able to focus on anything but Gabriel and my father and the dilemma before me.

Agent Lewis's business card feels like a brick sitting in my purse.

What if it's only a matter of time before the FBI makes their case against Gabriel? The Easton brothers could end up at Fulcort without any help from me, and then I've lost my chance to secure a second chance at life for my father.

Am I a terrible daughter for having not jumped on this opportunity the moment I had it?

But then all I have to do is think about Gabriel—that playful smile, the way my heart skips when I see his name appear on my phone, the way his hands feel on my skin, the safety I feel when I'm folded within his arms—and thoughts of conspiring against him make me want to vomit. I can't do it to him.

Is it because I'm afraid of what he'll do to *me*? Yes, there is that, and it's a twisted notion when I spend any amount of time thinking about it. But I'm beginning to think it has less to do with fear of retribution and far more to do with how I feel about him.

I've fallen in love with Gabriel, that deplorable man who bribed me to sleep with him. Who has given me everything I've asked for.

Whose heart I seem to have won.

I *can't believe* I've fallen in love with him. He's a criminal, and not just a petty thief or the "got into a drunken bar fight and hurt someone worse than I intended" brand. And yet I find myself making enough justifications for the things he's done to be able to see past his wrongdoings to the man he is beneath.

And that man? He makes me laugh; he makes me cry out with pleasure; he makes me enjoy life again.

"Would you just go already?" Michelle hisses.

I sigh reluctantly. "Fine." With whispered "excuse mes" and cringes of apology past four people, I exit our row in center orchestra and focus on my stride up the long, dimly lit aisle, the numerous martinis making my head light and my heels wobbly.

Moe appears from the shadows to trail me, his movements sleek. How he secured a corner to stand in is beyond me, but I'm sure it involved plenty of green dollar bills.

"Stay here with Michelle. I'll be back in a minute. I'm just going to the restroom," I explain, trying to keep the irritation from my voice.

He ignores me, speeding up to push through the door ahead of me, his head swiveling this way and that to check our surroundings, as if there might be a threat waiting in the corridor.

I roll my eyes and silently pray they find this murderous uncle soon so I can lose the pleasure of my chaperone.

That thought is immediately followed by a stomach-spasming question: what happens when they do find him? What will Gabriel do? What role will he play in retribution for Felix and Finn's deaths?

Will he pull the trigger?

That thought doesn't elicit the same harsh reaction that discovering a bloody T-shirt in Gabriel's trash can brought about, when I convinced myself he was out burying bodies while I slept soundly in his bed.

Have I so quickly become desensitized to what Gabriel is capable of?

Or am I tired of being a victim in this shitty world? Have I become attracted to the power Gabriel holds, the semblance of control over what happens in my life that he seems to provide?

A part of me doesn't care who does what, as long as the threat is gone. This uncle killed four innocent people. He tried to kill us, and it sounds like he'll try again. It's either us or him who survives. I choose us.

Shit. Gabriel and I are an "us."

Moe is still hot on my heels as I reach the women's restroom. I pause at the door and muster all my courage to glare at him in warning. "You're staying *out here*." There's no way this guy is standing outside the stall to listen to me pee.

Thankfully Moe doesn't argue, settling in with his back to the wall to study the empty hallway.

Beyond a long, narrow hallway and a second door is the most luxurious restroom I've ever been inside. It's empty of people. I scan the marble floors and elaborate stone sinks before ducking into a stall—each one a private little room with a full door. Temporary relief overwhelms me as I empty my bladder of my liquid dinner. I wish I'd been able to stomach a bite or two of that impressive-looking meal. Maybe then Ralph the angry chef wouldn't have had reason to cause that embarrassing scene. Then again, it led to Gabriel and Caleb meeting the hotel owner ahead of schedule. They were still talking—and laughing—when Michelle and I left for the show. By the grin on Caleb's face and Gabriel's playful wink, I got the vibe that the impromptu meet-and-greet might set things up nicely for their future business conversations.

Gabriel wasn't joking about buying this hotel and turning a new leaf, getting away from the dirty side of the Easton empire. Those good intentions must account for *something*, right?

I stare at my clutch purse in my hand, Lewis's card buried depth within, as my conscience tries to work through this mess.

Maybe the FBI has nothing on them. Maybe she's fishing, hoping I'm her meal ticket to making her case. She certainly seems willing to risk my life in order to succeed with that.

I'll wish Diego had finished me off.

Dad's warning to not do anything risky rings in my

head. Working as an FBI informant against the very man I'm falling hard for isn't just risky; it's insane.

I should just destroy this business card and remove all temptation. Trust that Justin DeHavilland will work legal magic and reverse this murder conviction. Believe that Gabriel and Caleb are going legitimate, that they'll change. And let myself dream about a future with Gabriel, as slim and idiotic as that may be. Flutters stir in my stomach at the thought of that.

Before I can talk myself out of it, I fumble through my wallet, digging the card out from its hiding place. I tear it in half, and then quarters, and I keep tearing until it's nothing but a tiny pile of paper, the ink on the scraps a puzzle no one will ever piece together. I dump it into the bowl and flush the contents.

A heaviness lifts from my chest, and I know that, while that might not be the smart thing, it's the right thing for me. I don't want any part in sending Gabriel to prison. In his twisted way, he has helped my father and me more than anyone else has in my life.

With this newfound sense of relief, I exit the stall.

And stumble. Agent Lewis is leaning against the sink, drawing a fresh coat of lipstick over her full lips with precision. Her thick black curls are shiny and styled loose, framing her face.

I didn't hear anyone come in, but the stalls are well sealed and I was preoccupied. In part, by this fucking woman. How does she keep finding me?

I steal a panicked glance toward the exit, where I know Moe stands on the other side. The restroom was empty when I entered, so she must have passed him on the way in. Did he size her up and decide she was no threat to me? I mean, why would he suspect the attractive, curvy woman in a sexy black pencil dress at a Vegas Cirque du Soleil show is an FBI agent plotting to take down his employers?

But what the hell is she doing here? Wasn't one stealthy ambush enough for today? Has she been following us, just waiting for another opportunity?

I waver on the idea of leaving without washing my hands so I can avoid a conversation, but something tells me there's no avoiding this woman. She'll find me again. Next time could be with Gabriel around the corner.

My heartbeat is pounding in my throat as I choose the sink closest to her and fill my hands with soap. I grit my teeth, saying nothing, waiting for her to make her move.

"I *wish* I could bend my body like these guys," she murmurs, puckering her lips against the flattering deep plum shade.

I hesitate. "Same."

"Of course, they're probably all born double-jointed. How else do you explain the things they can do?" She snorts. "Ten years of yoga, and I still lose my balance on Downward Dog."

She's keeping it light, casual. She would have seen Moe on her way in. She recognizes the danger of serious conversation here.

I allow myself a soft sigh of relief as I rinse my hands. "Enjoy the show," I offer, drying off with a paper towel before crumpling it and dropping it into the trash can.

I turn to leave.

"So, have you considered my offer?" Her sharp dark brown eyes regard me through the reflection. "Are you ready to work with us?"

I give the door a pointed glare before hissing, "Are you trying to get me killed?"

A satisfied smile curls her lips. "So you're admitting that you know who Gabriel is?"

Shit. I swallow, taking a moment to steady my voice. "I'm saying, *if* he is who you say he is, then you're risking my safety by cornering me in the bathroom like this, especially with *him* outside." Granted, there's a long hallway and two doors between us but *still.*

She nods once, as if accepting my response, before shifting her focus back to applying another layer of color. It's all an act; her lipstick is already impeccable. "Gabriel and Caleb met with two men this afternoon, while you were at the spa. Vince and Merrick Perri."

A prickle of awareness dances along my spine. The FBI must be watching our elevator. "Okay?"

"They're known criminals and rivals of the Easton family." She cocks her head. "Did you see them when you went back to the suite?"

Something tells me she already knows I did. I shrug nonchalantly. "There were a couple guys there, but I didn't talk to them."

"Did you overhear any of their conversation?"

"No."

"Did Gabriel tell you what they were—"

"*No,*" I snap, louder than I intended. "I went to my room to take a nap."

Her eyebrow arches with incredulity. "I tell you that your boyfriend is a key player in the heroin and cocaine trade and you go upstairs to *take a nap*?"

"Yeah, I really wasn't feeling well after our little conversation. This one isn't making me feel too well either—"

"Why are you protecting him, Mercy? He nearly got you killed only twenty-four hours ago. Come on! You must know that was because of him?"

I press my lips together and stay mute.

Her features smooth over. "Look, I can see that you care about him. I get it. I've fallen for some unsavory men too. Take my advice though: it *always* ends, and the endings are never pretty. With a guy like Gabriel? Especially so." She pauses. "But if you *really* care for him, you'll work with me here. Before it's too late for him."

"What do you mean?" Is she saying the FBI is willing to protect Gabriel?

She presses her lips together as if deciding whether she should reveal anything. "The cartel has been making big moves lately. We have a string of murders that point to a growing turf war. Now two of the most powerful crime families on this side of the country are meeting together. I need to know why, and I need to know before more innocent people get hurt. People like Felix and Finn Walsh, and that pilot and flight attendant. They had young children, Mercy. Four, between the two of them." She watches me intently. "I think Gabriel is getting himself involved in something *very* dangerous. Something that could get him killed."

"I don't know anything about that," I answer truthfully as my heart begins to pound. Murders? A turf war? The fucking cartel? Every TV and movie I've ever watched that involves the cartel depicts ruthless savages who decimate entire families. Gabriel never mentioned anything to me about *any* of this. Is this what Caleb was referring to when he said his brother was getting in way over his head?

Earlier, he mentioned competition coming in to take over territories, and an attack.

Is Gabriel's uncle not the only danger? Is the cartel coming after him, too?

My fear spikes. I don't want Gabriel involved with *any*

of this. The sooner they can buy this hotel and disentangle themselves from that world their father raised them in, the better.

I swallow my hesitation, choosing my words carefully. "What about their father and their uncle?"

Lewis's eyes narrow. "What about them?"

"I mean, what if you could build your case against them?" *And leave Gabriel and Caleb out of it?*

"Depends. What do you know about them?"

I hesitate. Am I really doing this? Yes, I am, because four children lost a parent in a horrific way last night. "I know his uncle is behind the plane exploding. You could get him for murder, right?"

Something flashes in her eyes. A sense of impending victory, perhaps. "If I had evidence. Do you have that?"

I shake my head.

"Can you get me some?"

"I don't know." I peer over my shoulder, expecting Moe to stick his head in at any moment. Is he wondering what's taking me so long? Or is he giving me privacy on account of my earlier "illness"? "Look, you need to leave. *Now*. You're putting me in danger."

Agent Lewis lowers her voice. "You're not the only person feeding us information, Mercy. We *will* find out what they're up to. We *will* bring their entire empire down. You have the chance to be on the right side of this. I have someone in place, ready to help protect you."

"Who? Where?" How is *anyone* going to get past Farley's military-grade guards to protect me?

Unless one of Farley's guys is a fed.

"It's better you don't know. But I can't protect Gabriel without your help. I need you to find out what you can for me. Help me save Gabriel. And your father. You *want* to save them both, don't you?" There's a hint of desperation in her tone.

Alarms go off inside my head.

"Save Gabriel how? By putting him in prison for the rest of his life?"

She opens her mouth but then hesitates. "You don't think he deserves prison?"

He probably does, I want to say, but I care too much about him to help make it happen. Besides, I don't trust this woman. Every other angle she's tried so far hasn't worked. Now she's playing on my feelings. She doesn't give a damn about Gabriel or my father. Or me, given she's cornered me again, and so boldly, with Moe right outside.

"I already told you, I don't know anything. The only business calls Gabriel ever takes around me are from his nightclub manager. Now, stop approaching me. I don't want any part of whatever you're trying to drag me into." I move for the door, struggling to hide the fact that I'm shaking.

"It's interesting that Justin DeHavilland is representing your father's appeal case." She turns to face me, crossing her arms over her chest. The soft, crooning voice is gone. Now her forehead is furrowed, her caring façade cracking, her frustration with my stonewalling bleeding through. "How can you suddenly afford one of the top lawyers in the country?"

Justin must have filed the appeal paperwork already, and this bitch ferreted out the information. "He's doing it pro bono," I lie, hoping I haven't just dug a hole for him to fall into. It's one thing to lie to my father, but this is the FBI. They have ways of finding things out.

"The same law firm that represents crime boss Vlad Easton is taking on pro bono cases? That's hard for me to believe."

I steal my voice. "It doesn't matter what you believe, does it?"

Her lips twist. "You want to know what I think?"

"Not especially." I'm desperate to get away from this woman, and yet my feet are rooted in place.

"You're a *beautiful* woman, Mercy. And Gabriel is a good-looking man with *a lot* of money and power." She takes a step forward, and then another. "I think you attracted Gabriel's attention in Fulcort, learned who he was, and saw an opportunity to get something out of it."

I struggle to school my expression as my heart hammers in my chest. *Not exactly how it happened, but you're not too far off, Agent Lewis.*

Her eyes flit over my features as if searching for a tell to suggest she hit the mark. "Or maybe it was your father who saw an opportunity and put you up to it."

"My father would never do something like that," I throw back before I can bite my tongue.

Her perfectly drawn eyebrow twitches. "So *you* saw the opportunity then. And you've secured protection and a fancy new lawyer for your father in exchange for... what exactly?" Her lips part with a broad smile. There isn't so much as a hint of lipstick smeared across her perfect white teeth. *Bitch.* "You must be one hell of a lay to keep a man like Gabriel Easton interested."

My cheeks flush. "You're wrong."

But she's on a roll now. "When did you two begin dating? Was it before or after Diego Montoya almost killed your father?" She steps closer, into my personal space. "Did you know Gabriel was going to have Diego killed, or was that just a bonus to your arrangement?"

"He killed himself," I manage around a hard swallow.

She goes on as if I haven't spoken, her eyes narrowing.

"Or maybe Gabriel had Diego taken out of because *you* asked him to. Do you think your hands are clean because you didn't tie the belt around his neck?" She shakes her head slowly. "That's still conspiracy to commit murder, Mercy. Do you have any idea what kind of sentence that carries?"

My head starts spinning as Agent Lewis gets closer and closer to the truth, and my guilt threatens to swallow me up. "I never asked Gabriel to do *anything* to Diego. You're just speculating," I say, my voice barely a whisper. But I did ask him to protect my father. Deep down, I knew what that might mean. And after the fact, once I deduced what Gabriel must have orchestrated—a staged suicide—I didn't care. I was happy the threat to my father was gone. I rationalized his death.

In some ways, I'm as much a monster as anyone in the Easton family.

"It's such a waste, to see a young woman like you, with her whole life still ahead of her, throwing it all away. And for what? A well-used dick that'll only get bored of you soon. Or is it the sparkly baubles?" She nods toward my hand, where countless diamonds wink back beneath the vanity lights. "Once Gabriel finds a new plaything and this deal is off the table, maybe you can use that to cover some of your legal fees. Not that it'll get you off. I doubt Gabriel has any connections at Regent to protect you, anyway. You've heard about the women's prison, right? You think Fulcort's bad?" She smiles. "Wait until you end up in there for—"

The outer door to the restroom creaks open.

"—seriously, *love* the ring," Agent Lewis switches to a loud, playful tone midsentence, reaching for a paper towel and pretending to dry her hands just as Moe rounds the corner. Under her breath, she whispers the softest, "Help yourself before it's too late," and then she spins and sashays toward the door.

Moe stands in the center of it, blocking passage with his lean but muscular body, his face stony as he considers her.

"Excuse me." Agent Lewis's lips press into a tight smile.

He stares her down for one... two... three beats—long enough that the air in the fancy restroom grows dense and I find myself holding my breath in trepidation—before he shifts to the side.

She exits briskly, as if nothing out of the ordinary just happened. She seems fearless, but I wonder if her heart is hammering in her chest as hard as mine is right now.

"Who was she?" Moe asks.

"Nobody. Some woman who liked my ring." I peer down at my hand, at the "sparkly bauble" Agent Lewis claims Gabriel used to buy me. Joke's on her though; I can't be bought with diamonds. Now, dangle a fancy lawyer and a scary prison fighter named Chops in front of me, and that's a whole other story.

Agent Lewis was guessing. That's all that was. She was throwing shit out to see what might stick. The problem is, her aim is too close for my liking. How long before she has proof to back her hypotheses up? Before she has something to hold against me, to force me into doing her bidding?

I feel Moe watching me. "Do you always barge into the women's restroom like this?" I ask, setting my palms on the counter to brace myself while my legs shake.

"You were taking a long time," he says, deadpan.

"So what?" I snap, my panic flaring.

"Why are you so scared?" he asks, undeterred by my sharp tone.

"Because you make me uncomfortable." I attempt irritation at his questioning—it's the most I've ever heard him say

—but all I hear is the shake in my voice. I check my reflection and find a pale, wide-eyed version of myself staring back. He's wrong, I'm not scared. I'm *terrified.* Agent Lewis has clearly decided I'm the golden snitch in the Easton case, and she's intent on catching me.

I feel as trapped and helpless as the day my father was sentenced. The urge to scream overwhelms me.

But that was reckless of her, approaching me the way she has today, first at the spa and now here, with Moe hovering. What the hell was she thinking? She says she can protect me? She will literally be the death of me if this doesn't play out the right way. Namely, if Gabriel and Caleb get the impression that I'm working with her to bury them.

And the way Moe is sizing me up, he already has his suspicions. It's only a matter of time before he shares those with Gabriel.

Unless *he*'s the FBI protection Agent Lewis is talking about.

That fleeting thought passes through a second time, slowing, giving itself a chance to gain purchase. Could a guy like Moe have worked his way into the Easton's organization? It would have taken months. Years, even. How long has he been with Farley? Why does Farley trust him? How do you even end up being security detail for a crime family?

My mind begins spinning, searching for ways that this could make sense.

Farley said Moe asked to be on my detail, specifically. Why would he do that?

Someone has been feeding Agent Lewis details of my whereabouts all day today—exactly where I'd be and when —so she could slither in and put pressure on me.

The fact that she approached me with Moe so close by? The way she marched past him, just now?

I might be totally wrong. I might be completely off-base.

But what if I'm *not* wrong?

"You look ill," Moe states in that cool, robotic voice.

"Yeah, I guess I'm still fighting off whatever bug I caught," I mumble, eying him steadily. He's built, his movements are sleek, he says very little but he's always, listening.

His lips twist. "You sure that's all it is? Or is there something you need to say?"

My heart hammers inside my chest. Do I confront him about it? Do I tell him that I know?

The door swings open, and Michelle strolls in, her gold dress shimmering with each step. She spares Moe a wary frown before turning her attention to me. Her eyes widen. "Oh my God, Merce! What's going on? You're pale as a corpse!" Her brow pinches with concern as her attention flips from me, to Moe, and back to me. She must sense the tension hanging in the air between us. "Come on." She tucks her phone into her clutch, and reaches for me with her free hand, a sour expression filling her face. "Let's go back to the suite."

"We can't. They're meeting with…." My excuse drifts.

"*With*?" Michelle pushes.

Someone dangerous.

Someone Gabriel doesn't trust.

He said there are things in play that I have no clue about. Does Gabriel know about the FBI circling them? Does he suspect Moe? Would he send Moe with me if he did? What if he has no idea? What if Lewis is telling the truth, and they're close to taking them all down? A flash of my future hits me then—of Saturdays in Fulcort, visiting my father *and* Gabriel.

The thought feels like a punch to my heart.

I can't do this anymore.

I need to tell Gabriel everything *now*.

I need to come clean with him about Agent Lewis.

And I need to warn him in case he's heading into a trap.

"...Don't worry. When they buy this hotel, we can see as many shows as we want. Until then, you need to get over this bug." Michelle rubs my forearm as she prattles. "Come on. We're going back to the suite before you collapse."

"Gabriel and Caleb—" Moe begins, but Michelle cuts him off.

"Gabriel would want her resting in bed if she's this sick, *wouldn't he*?" She glares at him, daring him to challenge her.

He studies me with those penetrating eyes for what feels like an eternity. Finally, he checks his watch, sighs heavily, and nods.

TEN
GABRIEL

"I DON'T KNOW what that fucker's been smoking, but he's not getting anywhere near that kind of coin for this place. Especially not when people know he's got creditors waiting around the corner with their hands out." Caleb slams his fist against the button to close the elevator door. His giddy spirits at the beginning of our conversation with Bruce Cohen soured quickly when he steered the conversation toward our interest in buying the Mage and the little man laughed in his face. Then he threw out an astronomical number, assuming we'd balk at it.

The truth is, I *did* balk. It would put a serious dent in our coffers. "He probably will get it, creditors or not. This is prime Vegas real estate. We'd have to be idiots to believe he doesn't have a bunch of suits breathing down his neck on the daily to scoop it up."

"Then why hasn't he sold already, huh? Why keep this headache? All he did the whole time we were talking was bitch about it!"

"Because look at the fucking guy! He's five-foot fuck all and one hundred pounds soaking wet. Being a Vegas casino owner gives him cred. It's the only way he gets pussy without having to buy it."

"That's a lot of work for pussy," Caleb mutters, fidgeting as the elevator climbs. "Then again, look who I'm talking to. The king of doing stupid shit all in the name of pussy."

"Shut the fuck up."

Caleb smirks, enjoying the sly dig at me. "I'll work on Cohen some more later."

"*If* he shows up." Through gritted teeth, Caleb invited Bruce to our place later tonight, dangling high-end booze and women as bait.

"He'll show. Trust me. He knows he can't keep this place, bleeding money the way he is."

"And who says *we* won't bleed money, too? *All* our money! We don't know what we're doing. Empire is a sandbox in a kids' playground next to this."

"Which is why we have Mike. *He* knows Vegas."

"He *better* know Vegas, or we'll end up in the poorhouse and I'll never let you hear the end of it." I'm all for brass balls-level confidence, but maybe we're biting off more than we can chew this time around. Something Mercy said earlier lingers in my mind. "You know, maybe we should think about a partnership, to hedge our investment."

"A partnership?" Caleb turns to frown at me. "With fucking *who*? *Who* do you actually trust *that* much, besides me? Because I don't trust anyone besides you, bro."

"What about Merrick and Vince?"

"*Merrick* and *Vince* Perri? You want to go into business with the fucking *Perris*?" My brother glares at me with so much disgust, it's as if I suggested we venture into human trafficking.

"Not the Perris. *Just* Merrick and Vince. They said they were looking at investing in a club or something."

"This is not a club, Gabe."

I roll my eyes. "Yeah, no shit."

"So let them go buy a snooker dive or a titty bar. Whatever gets their rocks off and makes them feel like legit businessmen. They're not cutting their teeth at our expense."

"We're already in a partnership with them," I remind him. One that could get us killed if any of us talk.

"Yeah, well, the clock is already ticking on that one. Plus, we don't have to deal with them on the regular. Can you imagine those two in our faces every day? Answering to Merrick, with his snotty little bitch attitude?" He snorts. "We wouldn't last two weeks before I'd beat the shit out of him."

I smirk. "Or he beats the shit out of you."

"Not a fucking chance. End of discussion."

I sigh. "Yeah, fine. For now, anyway." I check my watch. It's twenty minutes to ten. Our little chat with Bruce went longer than expected, leaving us little time to prepare for the larger Perri clan. "I got a call from Diesel just before dinner. Three of Puff's guys are missing. Cousins of his."

Caleb curses. "Cartel?"

"Assume so."

"Dad's going to *love* hearing about that van of body parts," he mutters dryly. The elevator doors open to the pulse of dance music and female laughter. Loitering around the bar are three Vegas showgirls, all in sparkly silver costumes that barely cover their assets. I spot three more dipping their toes into the pool.

Normally, my dick would twitch at the sight. Now, I merely shake my head at my brother. "Are you kidding me? We agreed to waiting until *after* for your entertainment to arrive." Thank God Mercy isn't here to see this. He's making me a liar.

"We didn't agree to shit. You talked, I didn't listen. America, the beautiful!" Caleb throws his arms out as he steps off the elevator, heading for the blond—America—in the silver thong bikini. He always spends at least one night humping her on every trip to Vegas. I don't know why I expected this time to be different. Oh, right, because he's been busy humping my girlfriend's best friend.

Caleb embraces America in a bear hug, lifting her off the floor to spin her around. "How long has it been?" comes his muffled question, his face buried in her perky tits.

"Three *long* months." She coils long dancer legs around his hips. Her ass is a beautiful thing, ripe for bouncing quarters.

"That sounds about right."

"What happened to your face, baby?" Her flawless forehead furrows with her pout as she peers down at him.

"It's nothing. Just a little disagreement. I'm still pretty though, right?"

She giggles, smoothing her palms across his jawline. "*So* pretty."

He grins slyly up at her. "I missed,you."

"I missed you, too. I brought some friends, like you asked."

"I see that. Thank you."

Mercy is going to be so pissed if America's still here when they get home. I feel an unexpected flare of anger on her behalf. But this was inevitable. Caleb wasn't about to settle down with Michelle. He's incapable of committing to *anyone*.

Besides, with T minus twenty minutes to being in a room with Camillo and Miles Perri, the best place for

Caleb's head to be is buried in a woman's breasts. Otherwise, he'd be pacing the suite like a caged lion with a loaded gun, ready to attack.

I pass the ladies with nothing more than a passing glance—the brunette on the far left looks vaguely familiar; I'm pretty sure I fucked her the last time I was in Vegas—to reach Farley, standing sentry by the games room, keeping everyone in and out. "All set?"

He nods in answer.

"How long has the entertainment been here?"

"They just got here. Caleb told us to let them up."

"Of course he did." I know this is really about Vince's dig earlier at our lack of pussy. My brother saw it as a challenge. He's a Neanderthal like that.

"We took their phones and patted them down for any wires," Farley confirms. "None of them have left my sight."

I sigh. The last thing we need tonight are witnesses. "Get rid of them before Camillo and Miles arrive. Send them to the club. The concierge should be able to get them a VIP table. *No one* comes up until after." I know how Caleb rolls. This group is the first of many for the night. He had serious debauchery planned for last night, back when Felix and Finn were supposed to be here. Now that they're gone, he'll be dialing it up ten notches in their honor.

My stomach clenches with the thought of our friends. It reminds me that we still have another big problem besides this impending meeting with the Perris. With that in mind, I take the stairs two at a time, up to my bedroom, sliding my burner phone out of my pocket on the way.

Stanley answers on the second ring. "Nothing yet," he says by way of greeting, his voice gruff. "I had a lead, but turned out to be a dead end."

"Where the fuck are they, then?" I kick the door shut

with my heel, my frustration mounting. We've already turned all of Peter and Vic's usual spots, and Stan is tracking their credit cards. "Maybe Bane already got hold of them." If that's the case, it's a toss-up whether we'll find them or not, and in how many pieces. It all depends on Vlad's directive—make an example of them or make them disappear without a trace. Bane's skill with either is unparalleled.

"I think we have to start assuming the worst-case scenario. I haven't been able to confirm anything, but it's a possibility."

"Shit." Bane finding them would be best-case. Worst-case is that Peter has gone running to the Feds for their protection. And the only way the Feds will give them that is if he gives them something.

Namely, us. That sneaky fucker knows enough to put us away for life and could probably do it in a way so as to leave his own business interests intact.

Tension trickles down my spine. "If that's the case, you need to find that safehouse." Caleb will swallow a bottle of anthrax before spending a single night in Fulcort. I can't say I'd be too far behind him.

"Already scouring. But you've got a bigger problem right now, Gabe."

A bigger problem than my murderous uncle trying to kill us? "What's that?"

"My source tells me that the Feds have a CI on you."

"Yeah. Fucking Peter."

"Nah. Someone with you right now."

My stomach drops. "What do you mean? Who?"

"Don't know. All they said is this person's firmly in place and feeding them intel."

"*In place?*" That must mean they're with us here, in

Vegas. I pace around the bed, wracking my brain. We're fucking surrounded by possible traitors.

A six-man security team.

Merrick and Vince Perri.

Mercy.

She wouldn't do that to me... Would she?

Fuck. What if she would?

A hollow, sickly ache stirs in my chest.

"Is it male? Female?"

"Don't know."

"Well, fucking find out!" I bark.

"I'm working on it!" Stanley barks back. He's one of only a few who dare, and he knows he'll always get away with it because he's the best at what he does, and we need him far more than he needs us.

I take a deep, calming breath.

"Just watch yourself, and make sure that insane brother of yours doesn't do anything crazy with witnesses around."

"Yeah." I push aside thoughts of Mercy betraying me for the moment. "Did you get any leads on surveillance around the airfield?" One of those cameras *must* have caught something.

"Everything was seized before I could get to it. Still working on my contact inside."

My anger flares. As if the Feds are going to do anything productive with evidence from those video feeds. They're just as likely to sit back with bowls of popcorn and watch with glee as our family takes each other out. "Okay. Call me with an update in the morning."

I end the call with Stanley, my fist clenching around my phone, a tornado of emotion erupting inside me.

Caleb asked me earlier who I trust.

The truth is, I trust Mercy. Talking to her just comes

naturally to me. I can't help myself. I've told her things about our family that I've *never* told anyone else. I've told her things Caleb would beat the shit out of me for spilling.

The shit she knows? She could throw it like chum into the water to draw in the Feds like sharks. She could bury us, if she wanted to.

But I've given her *everything* she's asked for, and then some. Has it not been enough?

Am I just a fucking chump in all this?

If Mercy's informing for the Feds...

I'll deserve everything that's coming to me, I think to myself bitterly.

My phone rings. The last thing I want to do is talk to another person, but there are too many balls in the air to ignore a call, especially from Donny. That's three calls from him in the last twenty minutes. The first two I missed while we were working on Bruce Cohen. That's worthy of an answer. "What do you want?"

"You told me to let you know if anyone tried reaching out to Vlad through the guards," he says over the buzz and metal clang of prison doors closing sound in the background.

My pulse skips a beat. I hadn't expected anything. "Who? When?"

"Peter, about an hour ago, through Anthony."

Anthony Fasilli. A lowly wannabe-mobster guard that my father has tucked in his pocket. He doesn't have much clout around Fulcort, but I swear the guy would shave my father's saggy balls with tender loving care if Vlad so desired. Peter knows that. No wonder he went to him when he couldn't reach him by phone.

"What'd the message say?"

"That they weren't behind the hit."

I snort. "Yeah, bullshit."

"That's what the message said."

"Nah, I meant... Never mind. Did he say anything else?"

"Just that it wasn't them, and that Vic and Alexei have nothing to do with the other thing."

So Peter's accepted that his days are numbered, regardless, and is begging my father to spare his idiot sons. The psycho has a heart after all, however small and shriveled it might be. Too bad he didn't show as much consideration for his nephews when he tried to kill us. Dad won't let that go.

I pinch my nose, feeling the beginnings of a throbbing headache forming behind my left eye. "What was my father's response?"

"Radio silence, as far as I know."

Which is as good as a kiss of death, coming from my father. Even if Peter's telling the truth about the bomb, he still betrayed him.

"Let me know if anything else comes through." I end the call before Donny has a chance to respond, my mind swirling.

I dare to let myself consider the possibility that Peter is telling the truth, that it wasn't him who blew up our plane. I allow myself a moment to embrace that possibility. My thoughts quickly head down a dark and disturbing path. That crazy fuck has never denied a hit in his life. In fact, he's always worn them with a badge of honor. When he torched Perri's restaurant, inadvertently killing Camillo's mother, he strutted around with his chest puffed out. When he took our shifty turncoat cousin on a one-way trip out to the desert, he described with pleasure how the guy pissed his pants begging for his life.

That he's not owning up to this now sounds a few alarm bells.

If it is true, then it puts us right back to square one with possible guilty parties: the cartel or the Perris.

And the plane wasn't this cartel's MO.

What if, like my ever-suspicious brother suggested from the start, this is all one big fucking setup by the Perris to officially wipe the Eastons off the map? What if we're a bunch of fools, falling for Merrick and Vince's act, rolling out a red carpet to invite the wolves in? Has our father, with his idiotic push for an alliance, led us like fucking sheep to slaughter?

I check my watch. The wolves are set to arrive any minute. Everything is going to shit and fast. I need to talk to Caleb *now*.

Pausing long enough to fish another clip for my gun out of my bag, I throw open the door.

And startle at the sight of Mercy standing on the other side, her hand midair as if reaching for the doorknob.

ELEVEN
MERCY

Five scantily clad women in silver sequin showgirl costumes strut past us and into the elevator as we step out. They're giggling—drunk, is my guess—and they barely spare us a glance.

"You've *got* to be kidding me," Michelle mutters, her emerald green eyes locked on the terrace. She looks ready to vomit.

I follow her gaze and my stomach drops. *I*'m ready to vomit, too.

A man sits on the couch ahead with his legs splayed, his black pants bunched around his thighs. From this angle, it's impossible to tell whether it's Caleb or Gabriel because of the topless blond woman riding his lap.

Just the possibility that it might be Gabriel—that he could look me in the eye and spew all kinds of lies about how he feels about me—causes a sharp, stabbing pain in my chest. Am I throwing away a chance to save my father for a man like *that*?

Farley stalks over, sparing a heavy glare for his right-hand man before turning to me. "Gabriel asked that all guests visit the club for the next hour. We can get you on the VIP list—"

"I'm not a *guest*, and I'm not going to the fucking *club*," I snap, my anger flaring. "Is that *him* out there?" I stab the air with my finger.

Farley and Moe exchange a glance. "No, ma'am."

Overwhelming relief swarms me, followed by pity for Michelle. The delusion of a charming Caleb has been officially cracked. I feel bad for my best friend, but frankly, it's for the best. She doesn't need to fall in love with an Easton and have the FBI breathing down her neck, pumping her for information. It's not fun. I can now officially speak from experience.

"Where is Gabriel?"

"In his bedroom."

My stomach does another swan dive.

Is he alone? I open my mouth, but I can't bring myself to ask the question.

Charging past Farley, I storm up the stairs. Moe is hot on my heels.

Just as I reach for the doorknob, the door flies open.

TWELVE
GABRIEL

MERCY LETS out a small squeal of surprise and jumps back.

"What the *fuck* are you doing here!" I snap, my mind in overdrive as I take in her beautiful face. *Have you betrayed me to the Feds?*

My gut rolls at the thought.

Moe stands behind her. I glare at him, not bothering to guard my tone. "What *the fuck* is she doing here?"

"She wasn't feeling well," he answers in that cool, unbothered tone, as if I hadn't given him explicit instructions to keep her away. As if I'm paying him to use his goddamn discretion.

Mercy's mouth hangs open for a few beats, as if I just slapped her. But then she clears her throat. "What's wrong? You don't want me here for your important meeting with your showgirls? I'm sorry, am I hampering your style, you *fucking pig*?" Her voice cracks over her words, fire in her eyes as she searches the room behind me.

She's looking for a woman, I realize.

Ah, shit. The girls. They must still be downstairs.

I can't help the laugh that escapes me, despite the tense

situation. Those women are the *last thing* on my mind, but Mercy's right to be angry. If roles were reversed and I came home to find her with a bunch of men after she insisted she was having a girls-only night in, I'd shoot first and ask questions later.

And Mercy *is pissed.*

Pissed is good, though. There's no way she's the confidential informant with the level of rage she's channeling over just the suspicion that I'd be cheating on her. I don't know who it is, but it can't be her.

Relief slams into me. I would throw her onto our bed and prove to her how much I'm not thinking about the other women, if I didn't have this other pressing dilemma. "Mercy, I don't have time for this right now—"

"You're making time, you asshole!" She storms into the bedroom and shoves me back with two hands against my chest and more strength than I expect, especially from a sickly woman. Throwing the door shut in Moe's face, she turns to focus on me, her eyes wild like I've never seen them before, glistening like she's about to burst into tears.

"Mercy, it's not what it looks—"

"Are you in love with me, Gabriel?" she blurts.

I falter. "*What?*" That question, I did not expect.

Tears begin streaming down her cheeks. "It's a simple question. *Are you in love with me?*"

Jesus Christ. I don't have time for *this* conversation. "We can talk about this later." Hopefully. If these walls haven't been turned into a Jackson Pollock painting, the medium being my blood. "Caleb invited the women. I haven't touched them. I don't want to touch them—"

"I know," she snaps, closing in on me. "Yes or no, Gabriel. I need to know, right now. Do you love me, yes or no—"

"Yes!" It comes out in a roar, my heart racing as I admit that to a woman for the first time in my life. "Why are you asking?" Why now?

Her shoulders sag, and all the fire disappears from her eyes, replaced by resignation. And fear. "Because the FBI is trying to use me to get to you, and I want to know if you're even worth throwing my life away."

THIRTEEN
MERCY

Gabriel listens to me, his jaw hard, barely blinking as I download everything Agent Lewis threw at me today. My words are a jumbled mess, barely coherent as they tumble from my mouth and tears stream down my cheeks.

Through it all, I can't miss the dark storm brewing within his eyes. "What have you told her?" he asks, his voice overly calm.

"Nothing. I swear! I played dumb. But she's figured stuff out. Or parts of things. She knows Diego didn't kill himself. She's threatening to charge me with conspiracy to commit murder."

"That'll go nowhere," he says dismissively.

"You don't know that—"

"Yes, I do. I'd never let that blow back on you. *Never*. I'd take the fall before I ever let that happen to you." He glares sharply at me, as if I've gravely insulted him just by questioning him.

I swallow. It's the closest to an admission that he had a man killed for me as he's ever given, and now he's saying he'd go to prison for it? He committed that crime for me, for my father. Diego was nothing to him. A nobody.

I don't know how I feel about this, except... protected.

I reach out to him and he takes a quick step back, out of reach. His expression is unreadable as he stares at me, and with each passing moment of silence, my body trembles harder.

"Say something, please," I finally manage, barely a whisper. I can't breathe as I wait for his reaction to everything I've told him.

"So, this agent cornered you at the spa today, and you're only telling me about it now?" he asks slowly, evenly. "Earlier, you pretended to be sick—"

"I wasn't pretending! I was sick! I felt like vomiting." My regret flares. I knew I should have told Gabriel right then and there.

"Why didn't you tell me?"

"Because it's the FBI! I freaked out."

"Or because you were considering her offer."

I open my mouth to deny that.

"Don't lie to me," he warns sharply. "We made a deal with each other, remember, Mercy? No lying."

The denial dies on my lips, unspoken as guilt hammers my chest.

He nods, more to himself. "So, this agent offered you a deal to get your father out in exchange for information to put me away."

I flinch. "Yes. But I didn't tell her anything—"

He raises his hand in the air between us, silencing me. His brow furrows in thought. Is he replaying our conversation from earlier? Is he remembering all that he's told me about Vince and Merrick, about the prison fight club, about his uncle trying to kill us? Is it enough to make him worry?

Is it enough to decide I'm a liability that needs eliminating?

He told me he loves me, though, I remind myself with a calming breath. He looked as surprised as I was when that admission escaped his lips.

But he told me that before I admitted to my secret rendezvous with Lewis.

Are men like Gabriel even capable of real love?

More importantly, are they capable of killing the women they love for self-preservation?

I swallow my nerves. I need to explain myself. "When she approached me at the spa, I didn't know what to do. I needed to think about it. About my father, rotting away in that cell for the rest of his life, and how likely it is that Justin can get him out. And then she scared me, telling me that you've killed witnesses before, that you'd kill me if you thought I was working with them. You wouldn't even think twice about it."

"And you believed her? You thought I could hurt you like that?" I don't miss the flinch that flashes across his face, as if my words stung him.

Despite my fear, warmth blossoms in my chest for this man. "After what you said about your uncle working with the FBI and your father putting a hit out on him... yeah, I guess I did."

He shakes his head, as if he's listening to my words but can't fathom what I'm saying. "It's not the same."

"How is it not the same?"

"Because I dragged you into my shit." He shakes his head again. "I wouldn't blame you for hating my guts for all that I've put you through. You didn't ask for *any* of this." He adds softly, more to himself, "But I guess you're all in now."

"I am." For better or worse, it seems. This time when I

reach for his arm, he doesn't step away, allowing me a chance to stroke his muscular forearm, tracing the map of veins. "I tore up the card she gave me, Gabriel. I flushed it down the toilet. I don't want any part of this, of anything bad happening to you. They're investigating you. You and Caleb. They're watching you right now. Here, in the hotel—"

"I know." He pushes his hands through his thick mane of hair as he begins to pace, sending it into disarray.

My jaw drops, though I shouldn't be surprised. Gabriel's proven time and time again that nothing is out of reach for him. "How are you so calm about this? I've been losing my goddamn mind!"

He smirks. "Stay a while. You'll get used to it."

"Or you could stop doing things that attract their attention," I mutter. "When did you find out?"

"About the tail? They've been on us since we turned onto the interstate. Apparently they've got a CI on us. We don't know who it is yet." His jaw ticks. "I was afraid it was you."

"It's Moe."

He stops to give me a doubtful look. "What?"

I drop my voice in the off chance that the bodyguard has his ear pressed against the door. "I think it's Moe."

"Nah." Grim amusement flashes across his face. "He's one of Farley's guys."

"No, I'm telling you. I think he's working with the FBI. Or he *is* the FBI. Lewis said she had someone in place who could protect me, and you heard Farley. He said Moe *asked* to be on my detail. Plus, she knew exactly where I'd be, both times. She risked talking to me in the restroom with Moe *lurking around*. Why would she do that, unless she wasn't worried about being caught by him?"

Gabriel opens his mouth, but then stops and frowns at the closed door. "He's only been with Farley a few months. Fuck, you might be right," he mutters, checking his watch. "I need you to stay here. I'm going to send Michelle in here, too. Don't tell her anything. You've seen how bloodthirsty these agents can get to make their case. They'll stop at nothing."

"I won't. I promise."

He turns to leave.

"Are you angry with me?" I hold my breath, waiting for his answer.

His jaw tenses. "Honestly? I don't know what I am, Mercy. Disappointed. Angry. Hurt. You can't hide shit like this from me. *Ever*. We can't work like that." I've never heard him so somber before.

"I know. I won't ever, again."

"That agent, though. I want to—"

"*Please don't* do *anything* to her. I don't want you committing any more crimes on my behalf."

He sighs heavily. "Listen to me very carefully. That agent doesn't have shit on you, because you haven't done a single thing wrong. Not one thing, you got it?"

I feel my head bobbing in agreement.

"She's desperate, and she's trying to scare you into complying."

"But she knows all about me. Where I work, that I went to school—"

"I could have paid for that intel and had it in an hour. She's got nothing, and she's grasping at straws. It was a stupid move on her part though. She didn't realize how smart you'd be. Or that you'd actually give a shit about me." A strange look passes over his face. "Stay in here, no matter what you hear. You understand?"

A prickle of unease slides down my spine. "Gabriel, what's going on?" He's far more tense than he was when I left him after dinner. Now that I think about it, he seemed on the way out and in a hurry when I stormed in here, tears in my eyes, demanding he profess his love to me. I'm getting the distinct impression something bad is about to happen. "Lewis said something about a turf war and the cartel—"

He shakes his head. "Just stay in here. And if anyone but me or Caleb steps through that door and they're not waving a badge—" He fishes out a handgun from the duffel bag on the dresser. Popping the clip out, he checks it before reloading. He spins the gun around in his hand deftly, holding it out for me. "—you point and shoot, got it?"

I accept it, the metal cool within my palm. I set it on the bedside table. "What are you going to do about Moe?"

"Don't worry, we'll get the truth out of him." I see the wicked gleam in Gabriel's eye that tells me I don't want to know any more details. "For now, though, I'm going to send him in here."

"What?" I glare at him. "I don't want that guy in here with me!"

"I can't have him anywhere near what's about to go down. Besides, I want you protected, and no matter what he is, he'll do that."

"I'm going to screw this up."

"Hey. No, you're not." He cups my jaw between gentle hands. "Tell me now, you're either all in or all out, babe."

"I'm in." I weave my fingers between his. "I'm all in, Gabriel."

"Okay. Then just keep pretending you're my pretty, clueless girlfriend until I come back." He hesitates, but then leans in to kiss me.

I return it eagerly, weaving my fingers through his silky hair to pull him closer to me.

"I've got to go," he whispers, breaking free after only a second.

An ache fills my chest. That kiss didn't feel the same. It was missing something I can't put my finger on. "Be careful," I warn him.

He heads for the door, pointing at the gun. "Keep that nearby, but don't shoot him. A body our hotel room will complicate things," he throws over his shoulder.

I study the gun on the table.

Is this what a life with Gabriel is really like?

FOURTEEN
GABRIEL

WHATEVER DISEASE IS EATING AWAY at Camillo Perri is doing a bang-up job, because he's nothing but a shriveled old white-haired man with a hunch in his shoulder, looking weeks from getting familiar with a six-foot-deep hole in the ground

Miles Perri, on the other hand? He's still the same motherfucker I remember from years past, only with more gray hair and pounds on his gut.

How satisfying would it be to put three bullets into that stomach? Stand over him while he writhes in agony, slowly bleeding out? It's been nineteen years, and I can't remember the sound of my mother's laugh anymore, except to remember that it was beautiful and soft.

I have to tell myself to relax my fists as I stroll down the stairs toward the main room, where Camillo and his four sons wait. Leo—who is only slightly younger than Miles—Merrick, and Vince stand together, off to one side and away from their older psycho siblings. Maybe that's their standard practice, or maybe that's to keep up this illusion that they're not all scheming to kill us.

Maybe that whole story about Miles going after Merrick's boyfriend was bullshit. How else is he standing in the same room with the guy now?

Fuck. I was happier when I was sure my uncle was the one trying to kill us. I actually like the two youngest Perris.

At least they didn't insist on bringing security with them.

From the corner of my eye, I note Moe hovering near the entrance to the games room with Farley.

Yeah, nice try. If Mercy's right and he is a CI, he'd love to be a fly on those walls.

I close the distance to them. "Where's Michelle?" I ask quietly.

"In her bedroom," Moe says, his eyes locked on Camillo and Miles.

"Okay. Get her into my room with Mercy, and stay with them. If *anything* happens to her, I will hold you personally responsible." *And no federal agency will be able to save you.*

He meets my threatening gaze and then, with a curt nod, takes off upstairs.

"Hey." I jerk my chin toward Farley.

The behemoth leans in and gives me his ear.

"How solid is Moe?"

Farley turns to glower at me, like I knew he would. I've never questioned the guys he brings in for protection. I've never had to. "Fucking solid. *Why?*"

I match his lethal look with my own. "Because I have intel that says he might not be."

I can hear Farley's molars grinding as he shifts his focus up the stairs to the second floor, where his golden boy just disappeared.

"We'll deal with him later. I don't want him anywhere near us tonight." With that, I head for the patriarch, extending my hand in greeting. "Sorry to keep you waiting."

Camillo dissects me with cloudy eyes, leaving me standing there like an idiot with my hand out for an awkward moment, but finally he accepts it. His skin feels like parchment paper. "It's been a while since I've had the pleasure of visiting Las Vegas." His voice is deceptively deep for such a frail-looking old man.

"Really?" Caleb's lazy gaze drifts to the terrace. The girls have all been sent away, to get liquored up before their return. "I can't seem to stay away for too long."

"Let's get this over with. I've got better things to do with my time," Miles mutters.

Caleb flashes a toothy smile that instantly puts me on edge. I've seen that smile before. It usually means he's about to lunge for a guy's throat. But instead he takes a step back and gestures toward the games room. "Please. Get comfortable."

Miles doesn't hesitate, doesn't defer to his father, he simply marches in. Huh. Look at him, taking the lead already, with his father still breathing. I wonder what he thinks of this "alliance."

Vince nods at me before taking up the rear, heading into the room.

"Where the fuck have you been?" Caleb snarls under his breath. Apparently double D tits in his face and a pre-meeting screw were not enough to ease his tension.

"Getting news from Fulcort."

His eyebrows arch in question. "And?"

"Told you this was going to be a waste of our time," Miles complains, rocking back and forth in the leather chair he's chosen at the poker table.

Arrogant prick.

"You trust me, right?" I murmur.

"Always, bro," Caleb answers without hesitation.

"Okay, then. Follow my lead, but don't take it too far." With a deep breath, I stroll in behind Caleb and pull the pocket doors shut.

And then I draw my Glock and press the barrel against Miles's right temple.

FIFTEEN
MERCY

"Do you think you can chill?" I ask, trying to focus on the mindless movie playing on the flatscreen and not on the potential FBI informant standing by the door, gun in hand, or the regret clawing at my insides. I should have told Gabriel sooner. Now that I'm on the other side of things, it's clear I shouldn't have been afraid to tell him. He's not a monster. Not to me, at least.

Michelle huffs—for the tenth time in half as many minutes—before continuing to pace the full length of the massive floor-to-ceiling window next to the bed. She was in the other bedroom when Moe tracked her down. He told her I needed to speak with her "right away." He didn't tell her that once she came in here, she wouldn't be allowed out.

I haven't asked if she was packing up her clothes to leave, but by the sullen expression on her face, that's where her thoughts are likely at. I can't blame her for being upset—finding Gabriel like that would have been crushing, even in the early days—and yet the shitstorm that's swirling in this room is already cloying without adding her tension.

She stops suddenly and turns to stare at me.

"What?"

"You *look* better." Michelle watches me intently. "Do you feel better?"

"Yeah. I think so." Divulging my secret to Gabriel has certainly lifted a weight off my shoulders.

"Okay, then, let's go out." She reaches for her clutch purse and phone that sits on the nightstand.

"We can't."

"We're in Vegas and dressed to go out. *Why not?*"

I suck back a gulp of water while I search for a suitable answer that doesn't divulge anything. "Gabriel wants me to stay here."

"And since when have you ever listened to him? *Especially* when you know he's down there with a bunch of dick swappers rubbing themselves all over him."

"He's *not doing that.* They're not even here anymore. He sent them away." He's busy facing off with the men who murdered his mother. My stomach tenses. I'm not sure which is worse. "And he didn't have anything to do with those women showing up here. That's all Caleb."

"Right. And when they go to the strippers, Gabriel only has eyes for the sports on the TV screens." She shakes her head at me, and I know what she's thinking: that I'm an idiot for believing Gabriel, a womanizer, wouldn't be partaking in his brother's arranged "entertainment" if I wasn't here to catch him.

Up until even a week ago, I might have doubted that as well. But things between us are shifting quickly. Time and time again, with his actions, with his words, with the fleeting gentle caresses at every turn, with every smile that touches his lips the moment we make eye contact, he's shown I'm in his thoughts as much as he is in mine—which is constantly, as of late.

Tonight, he admitted to loving me. I had to ask—to prod—but he didn't flinch. He didn't deny it.

Has Gabriel Easton ever told a woman that he loved her? I'd bet money the answer to that is a resounding never. But he's changing. The appalling man I met that day in the visitor lounge at Fulcort is not the same man whose lips find mine late into the night and as the sun rises for a new day.

Or maybe it's me who is changing. Maybe I'm warming up to this new dark world that has embraced me as one of its own and is saving my father.

Either way, Michelle's bitter opinion sparks an urge to bite back. "Look, don't get bitchy with me because Caleb showed you *exactly* who you already knew he was." Despite my scolding words, my anger flares. Why couldn't he just *not* be a fucking douchebag for two nights?

Her jaw tightens. "I can't sit here all night while he's screwing around with other women, Mercy."

"We won't. And they're not doing that anyway. They're too busy with—" I steal a glance toward Moe. "—some people. A meeting." *How much does he know?*

She wraps her arms around her chest as if cold. "Is it about buying this place?"

"I don't know. I think so." I avert my gaze as I lie.

"Those two hot men from that night at Empire are here. I saw them come in." She begins pacing again. "Maybe I should hook up with one of them and let Caleb walk in on that. See how he likes it."

"Caleb wouldn't give a shit." Knowing him, he'd watch. He might even join in. But I'd care. It's one thing for Caleb to dick around on her. But those two come from a family that has murdered women simply for being married to the wrong man. "Stay *far away* from them, Michelle," I warn.

"Oh, great. More mob guys?"

I glare at her.

"What? As if *he* doesn't know who he works for." She throws a hand toward Moe, dropping her voice to a dramatic whisper to add, "He could probably tell you where *all* the bodies are buried."

Shit. It'll be hard for me to play the clueless girlfriend with Lewis after this. "Gabriel is *not* the mob. There *aren't* any bodies buried. You don't know what you're talking about. Now, would you *please* just shut up?" My heart pounds in my chest as I steal another glance at Moe, to find his gaze shifting from me, to Michelle, back to me, his expression never cracking, never hinting.

How much intel has he fed to the FBI on them?

How badly has he betrayed Gabriel and Caleb?

Will it be the Eastons who punish him or Farley and his guys?

A frown flickers over Michelle's forehead, and I know what she's thinking—*they are basically the mob, Mercy, and we both know it.* We've talked about it more than once. I wish I could explain so she'd at least play along and not say something that will dig me deeper into this hole.

"Okay, fine, whatever. But can we please go to the hotel club while they're having their little 'meeting.'" She air-quotes the word. "We can take *him* for protection."

So Lewis can corner me again? No, thanks. I shake my head. "I'm not really in the mood for clubbing." I'm not leaving this penthouse without Gabriel by my side again.

"Seriously, Mercy?" She resumes her pacing, her tone full of exasperation. "It's bad enough I caught that asshole—"

"I *warned* you."

"Fine, yes, you did! And you were right. Is that what

you want to hear?" she snaps. "But can you put yourself in my shoes right now?"

"I know. I'm sorry." I'd want to leave, too.

She bites her bottom lip. "And now I'm trapped in here."

"In a penthouse suite," I remind her acerbically. "And you're not trapped—"

"Okay, fine then. You stay here. *I'm* going out." She grabs her purse and marches for the door.

Moe moves fast to steps in front of it, blocking her.

She stalls, waiting a few beats for him to move. When he doesn't, she demands, "Let me by."

"You need to stay here." He remains calm, unperturbed.

"You *can't* make me." She sets her chin with defiance, but the wobble in her voice betrays her confidence.

The corner of Moe's mouth twitches as he stares her down. Not only could he make her, but something tells me he'd enjoy it.

She must sense it too—her eyes dart lower, to the gun in his hand—because she backs up a step, and then another, her throat bobbing with a hard swallow.

"We could use some drinks, Moe. Do you think you could grab us some?" I ask in as polite a tone as I can muster.

The moment drags as he stares at me. I assume his silence is the answer, until he asks, "What are you drinking?"

"Martinis. Extra dry for Michelle."

"I don't make martinis." He reaches for the door. "But I can get you your vodka."

"Gin!" Michelle croaks. "Real martinis are made with *gin*."

Moe rolls his eyes but nods. With sleek movement, he's

gone downstairs, leaving Michelle and me alone.

"Mercy, what the hell is going on?" Alarm shines in Michelle's bright green eyes. "I'm getting the weirdest vibe, ever since we left the show, and now they won't let us leave? I'm scared."

I have little time to explain. "Listen to me carefully. You *can't* say anything about Gabriel or Caleb and their criminal stuff, okay? Not even as a joke."

"Yeah. I picked up on that. But what's going on?"

I hesitate. I promised Gabriel that I wouldn't tell her anything, but I also promised I'd keep up this clueless charade, and she's making that difficult. "We think Moe's an FBI informant," I whisper. "We think he's been feeding all kinds of information to the Feds."

Her jaw drops.

"Gabriel doesn't want him anywhere near the Perris, which is why he's up here, babysitting us." He also doesn't want us anywhere near the Perris, for reasons I'm not about to explain.

"Who are the Perris?"

"Another crime family. A really fucking horrible one. They're rivals, but they're forming some sort of alliance."

She releases a breath slowly, as if trying to process this without panicking. "An alliance to buy this hotel?"

"No. Not for that business. For *the other* one." I give her a pointed look.

She worries at her bottom lip as her gaze lingers on the closed door. "Why do you think he's an informant?"

"Because he's said and done some things...." I wave my explanation off. "Look, there's an agent after me."

"*After you?*" she squeaks.

"Yeah. She's threatening me, trying to get me to turn on Gabriel." I don't have time to get into the Lewis ambushes.

"And now Gabriel's gotten word about an informant, so it makes sense."

"So *Gabriel knows* there's an informant?"

"Yeah, His person on the inside told him."

Her eyes widen. "Like *in* the FBI? They have people in there?"

"Michelle, come on. Look who they are," I chastise, but then I remind myself that she's new to the Easton world. I've been living it for weeks. "They have people everywhere. They can get *anything* they want."

She begins pacing again, her arms wrapped tightly around her chest. "Does Moe know that they know yet?"

"No. But I'm sure he will soon enough."

"What are they going to do to him?"

"Take a wild guess." My stomach twists. I don't want this life for Gabriel. I want him away from it.

"Oh my God." She blanches as a flurry of panicked thoughts flash through her eyes. She's imagining the worst, and she's horrified by it. "I have to get out of here. *We* have to get out of here. Do you hear yourself? Do you hear what you're saying right now, Mercy? How can you be okay with this?"

"I'm not okay with it!" My blood begins to pulse in my ears. "This is just how things work in their world."

"What if the FBI has something on Moe, to force him into doing this? Have you thought about that, huh? That maybe he has no other choice! Maybe they're threatening his family!"

"Would you be quiet!" I hop off the bed and rush over to crack the door open. I can just make out the top of his cropped hair at the bar. I push the door shut. "Believe me, I get doing stupid, dangerous things for my family. Of *all* people, I get that better than *you* or anyone else."

Michelle flinches. "You're right. I'm sorry."

It's my turn to pace. "That agent threatened to charge me with conspiracy to commit murder if I don't give her what she wants."

"Murder! For who?"

Gosh, with my exams and all that's happened, I never had a chance to tell her. "That guy who was attacking my father in prison. He hung himself."

"Like, legit?"

"He hung himself," I reiterate, giving her a severe look. That is the official story, and I'll take everything else to my grave.

She bites her bottom lip in thought. "What all is this agent telling you?"

"That she knows my father doesn't belong in prison. She's willing to use him as leverage to get what she wants or let him rot in there if she doesn't. How fucked-up is that?"

"*All of this* is fucked-up. Has she promised you anything in return for your help?"

"Yes," I admit reluctantly. "She said she'd get my dad out of prison. Put us in witness protection or something."

"That's good, Mercy. You're going to consider it, right?"

"I *have* considered it. Why do you think I've been so sick to my stomach all day?" I saw the pain in his eyes when he realized I'd been weighing my options. Even recalling it now twists my insides. "I can't do that to Gabriel."

"But it's why you're with him in the first place. To get your father out. *Remember?*"

"I know, but... not anymore."

Her shoulders sink. "Oh my God. *No,* Mercy—"

"I'm falling in love with him," I admit quietly.

"No, you're not. You can't be! He's a fucking mobster!

And you barely know him!" There's a pleading tone in her voice. "No, this is some sort of sick Stockholm syndrome."

I roll my eyes. "This is *nothing* like that."

She closes the distance between us, dropping her voice. "You're protecting a guy who would *kill* you if he found out that you were working with the Feds."

"That's the thing... I was afraid of that, but I don't think he would hurt me."

"Oh my God. *Seriously?*" She thrusts a hand toward the door, as if Moe is still standing there.

I know what point she's making, but she's wrong.

"I trust him. And he trusts me." At least, I hope he still does.

"Yeah? I'll bet they trust Moe, too. Won't help him much soon, will it?"

"I guess not." What possessed Moe to turn rat, anyway? What do the Feds have to hold over him that would make it worth him risking his life? They *must* have something. "I don't want Gabriel to go to prison."

"That's where he belongs. Both of them do. They've had people murdered."

"Yeah. Bad people."

"*They're* bad people! Them! The Eastons!"

My anger flares. "Uh, hi, you were *just* banging Caleb this morning. Have you already forgotten? I'm surprised. I would have thought he'd be more memorable, with all his experience." Had Michelle not walked in on the bump-and-grind show, she'd be on her knees for him tonight, happily.

"Yeah, well... that's *obviously* over," she mutters.

I sigh. I knew something like this would happen, and I knew she'd take it hard, but she's *really* not handling it well. Then again, she's been off since last night. Given the dark and dangerous turn these past twenty-four hours have taken, I need to cut her some slack. "I don't know what to say except I'm sorry I ever introduced you guys." *Even though I warned you, repeatedly.* "Enjoy the rest of the trip on his dime, and then go home and never talk to him again."

She shakes her head. "I just want to go home. Now." She bites at her polished thumbnail—a rare sight for Michelle, who prides herself on maintaining a flawless manicure. "You've already been through so much because of your father. None of that was your fault. But this? Getting involved in this world? With this man? You're *choosing* this."

"You're right. I am." I'm choosing a life where I don't have to struggle, where I don't feel completely alone. In this life, I have some semblance of control, some power. But, really, I'm choosing Gabriel. "It's not going to be like this forever. He doesn't want to be a part of that world anymore. That's why they're looking at buying this hotel, so they can get away from it."

"Or so they have another source to funnel their drug money through." Her gold dress shimmers in the lamp light as she paces and judges, her voice laced with scorn.

My stomach pinches with her words, as they give voice to a worry that lingers deep inside. The fear that I'm a fool, buying an unlikely story because I want to believe in the twisted fairy tale.

"That's not what they're doing." Because I can't think that, in order for Gabriel and me to work. "It's not his fault they were raised into this world." I feel like I'm being attacked by my best friend. The urge to defend them, to make her see that they're not so bad, overwhelms me. "Look, it's like your father—"

She whirls around, her eyes wide. "My father is *nothing* like them."

I hold my hands in the air in a sign of surrender. "Yes, I know. But you know how he's always talking about how you're going to take over Banks Jewelry when he retires? And how you've worked there every summer since high school? It's never been a question that you and Lisa will take over." Her older sister manages the inventory, while Michelle is skilled in the people side of things.

"Yeah." She frowns warily. "So?"

"So, that's how Gabriel and Caleb have been raised."

"Except with guns, violence, drugs, and an utter lack of respect for life. Their friends died last night, and apparently it's business as usual."

"I'm not saying it's right or okay, but—"

The creak outside the door is the only warning before Moe reenters, two martini glasses brimming with liquid and olives. "Farley made them." He sets them down on the nightstand and then slides his gun from his pants and takes up his station by the door.

Michelle dives for hers and sucks half of it back in a single gulp.

Even Moe's eyebrow rises a notch.

"I'm going to the bathroom," she announces, setting the glass back down with a clink, her wary gaze on him. *Way to play it cool.* She hugs her purse to her chest as she strolls to our en suite, her hands trembling.

If she keeps this up, she's liable to tip Moe off that something's amiss.

What would he do if he caught on to our suspicions about him? If he knew his days, maybe even his hours, were numbered?

I eye the gun in his grip.

I know what *I'd* do. I'd find leverage. Something—or someone—to threaten in order to escape.

When I reach for my drink, I note how badly my own hand is shaking. I chastise myself for judging Michelle's frazzled nerves as I take long, slow sips, my gaze on the TV screen, my mind unable to follow the plot.

"What's taking her so long?" Moe asks suddenly.

Is she taking long? I frown. I've lost track of time. How long has she been in there?

He strides over to pound on the bathroom door.

A moment later it opens, and Michelle fills the doorway, scowling but still visibly rattled. "What? I'm not even allowed to pee now?"

He takes a step back, enough to let her squeeze by.

"I booked a rental car, Mercy." She swallows. "I'm driving back to Phoenix tonight."

I open my mouth to argue—making the drive alone through the canyon at night is a terrible idea—but then I falter. What's the point of her staying? This trip has been a disaster since the moment we stepped out of the cars at the airport, and it's been spiraling out of control ever since. Michelle will be miserable the rest of our time. I can't blame her for wanting to leave. "Okay."

"You should come with me." It's a last-ditch effort, and we both know it. Besides, Gabriel would lose his mind if I tried leaving, given his uncle is still out there and this agent is stalking me.

I shake my head. The crestfallen look that fills her face twists my chest.

"I'll leave a few dresses for you in the closet. Make sure none of his skanks borrow them." She eyes Moe warily.

"Let her go. *Please.*"

When he doesn't make a move to block the door again, she walks briskly out and across the hall to her room to pack.

Moe's penetrating gaze is on her the entire way.

SIXTEEN
GABRIEL

Caleb flashes me a "what the fuck" look but keeps his guns trained—one on Camillo and the other on Leo. I knew he'd back me up, and with his usual Wild West speed.

"Wait until I get my hands on you." Miles growls, glaring at me. "I'll rip your balls off and piss down your—"

"We can talk about your weird kink later. It won't do you or your loved ones"—Caleb waves the gun on Camillo in the air, as if a reminder—"any favors right now."

Miles's ugly mug splits with a grin. "You Eastons can't count too well, can you...?" His eyes flicker behind us, to where Vince and Merrick stand, each of them with guns trained on our skulls.

I steal a glance over my shoulder. Vince's face is as stony and unreadable as usual. I expected the move—he can't look like he's choosing us over his own flesh and blood—but the fucker even took his safety off to point his weapon at me. *Way to commit, buddy.*

Merrick, hidden behind Caleb's broad frame, offers me nothing more than a half-baked wink. His safety's still on, and I doubt that was an accident. They're not going to shoot us, but they have to keep up appearances.

I'm gambling on that belief, anyway. Right now, it feels like a pretty big gamble, the tension whirling in this room choking. Farley's heart would stop if he walked into this.

"From behind. Is that how you're gonna do me?" Caleb has the nerve to smirk as he taunts the youngest Perri.

Merrick flicks the safety off and cocks his gun, earning Caleb's chuckle.

You really have a death wish, brother.

If Camillo catches on to the not-so-subtle jab at his son's sexuality, his wrinkled face doesn't let on. "What is this little *display* about?" He eyes Caleb's gun like it's a bug needing a swat. I'm guessing a part of him wouldn't care if Caleb pulled the trigger on him. He's probably already got his plot picked out.

"Peter's saying he didn't set the bomb."

"Yeah, because he *never* blows up shit," Leo, the quiet one of the bunch, retorts.

"He loves blowing up shit," I admit. "But he never lies about doing it. So why would he lie now?"

"You couldn't get the truth out of him?" Miles smirks. "I overestimated you."

I want to punch the smarmy smile off his face, made worse by the fact that my gun is still on him and he doesn't seem to give a shit. I feel like a chump. "It was a message to my father. We haven't been able to locate him yet."

"So Peter, who betrayed your family once and is now in hiding, says he didn't try to kill you to protect himself, and you believe him," Camillo asks. "You automatically assume *we* are behind this?"

"The thought has crossed my mind, yeah." And for good reason. "It'd be one hell of a fucking coup d'état."

Miles shakes his head. "You came to *us*, remember?"

Actually, it was Merrick and Vince who showed up at Empire one night, unannounced, but my father is the one who put the word out, drew them in. Plus, I don't know how much the older Perris know about that first visit, so I keep my mouth shut.

"If we wanted you dead, you'd already be dead," Camillo says with the confidence of a man who has his gunsights trained on us daily. "Are we here so we can all die in this room together and give the federal agents loitering in the lobby something to clean up, or can we discuss how we're going to come together to deal with the cartel? They're gaining territory by the day. If we don't do something, soon enough there'll be nothing left of either of our legacies."

Behind me, I hear Vince's teeth gnash. It seems he hates talk of legacy as much as I do.

I steal a glance at Caleb, who gives an almost imperceptible nod.

Three... two... we slowly lower our guns. Merrick and Vince follow suit.

Miles grimaces like he's chewing on lemons, his leg twitching. He's itching to jump to his feet and attack, but he stays put, his squinty eyes locked on his father.

"We lost a sizeable delivery this morning on its way to Sacramento. They were waiting in the valley at the drop. Left the five Mambas sitting in a row with their heads in their hands and then set fire to the truck. Burned everything. The money, the merchandise. All of it."

"Burned the money, too?" Caleb whistles. "That's a big fuck you."

And it's got cartel written all over it. "How'd they get the drop location?" I ask.

"One of the Mambas. His MC thought he was shacked up with a hooker and a bottle of Jack for the night. Turns out he was spending it with the cartel, having his fingernails cut off one by one. His old lady found him in the garage with his arms and legs bound behind him." Miles swirls the shot of whiskey in his glass once before downing it in a gulp. "His balls were stuffed in his mouth. You know, like a pig on a spit with the apple?" He holds his hand up and mimes an apple being stuffed in his mouth.

Even Caleb cringes.

"And the Mambas wants nothing to do with transporting your product after that." I don't blame them. The MC signed up to mule product for big money, not get mutilated as mock feast day centerpieces by a bunch of psychopaths.

"It's a temporary setback. We'll deal with them." Camillo's lips purse, as if the words forming in his mouth are curdling. "But we are looking to build new relationships. We need other means of transportation and new routes."

"Let me guess, through our territory." Using our networks, which are arguably smarter and more efficient than a bunch of goons on motorcycles.

"It won't be your territory for long once Navarro sets his sights on you," Leo warns.

"Why would we ever agree to this?" Camillo isn't looking for a simple alliance. He's looking to invade. I may not want anything to do with the drug business, but my territorial back is up.

"We would compensate you."

"Fuck yeah, you would," Caleb counters, pushing his hands through his hair, sending it into disarray. "But so far all I'm hearing about is how we're helping you guys. This isn't an 'alliance.'"

I'll give it to my brother, he's doing a good job of selling the lie that he actually gives a shit if the cartel swoops in to take over, that he doesn't want out as bad as I do.

Camillo's eyes narrow as he studies my brother. "Where do you think your uncle is right now?"

"I don't know, but we'll find him soon."

"And we'll deal with him," I add, echoing the old man's earlier words.

"If he's not already in a safehouse, divulging all your deep, dark family secrets." Camillo's lips twitch. "He's been known to do that."

"Like I said, we'll deal with him." Nothing will stop Bane once he finds them, including the Feds. He's a wraith in the night.

"You need to make changes to your operation. We can help you with that. And the Mambas MC has charters all over the oast and a connection to guns. Once we get over this little hiccup, they'll be willing to offer their muscle and firepower for the common good."

"Even if the common good involves us and Puff's network?" The Black Mamba MC and Puff's gang have been at odds over territory for years, and those odds have found them in too many bloody showdowns to count. Them working together sounds about as likely as, well, us and the Perris.

"Business is business. And they don't want Navarro getting comfortable here any more than any of us do."

"So? Do we have an agreement?" Camillo pushes.

Caleb and I share a glance. It's smoke and mirrors. It doesn't matter what we agree to, because we're walking away from it all, and no Easton will be left to keep it going once Bane catches up with Peter and his sons.

But, by agreeing to this, we're effectively handing our

family's empire to the Perris—to Leo Perri, specifically. That is, until the cartel wipes him off the map. As much as I want out of the drug business for good, that's a prickly horse pill to swallow.

Regardless, this has to look legit.

"We'll get back to you. We're lying low until we deal with Peter. And I'll need to talk to Puff. See if this arrangement is copacetic for him." Once his missing cousins resurface—most likely in pieces— he'll be itching to form alliances with the devil himself if it means taking down Navarro's people.

Camillo nods. "You do that and reach out to Miles when you're ready."

"No. Our point of contact will be Merrick and Vince. For everything. Negotiation, communication. *Everything.*" Caleb's eyes narrow at Miles. "Them, and only them."

Miles snorts. "Nice try. I run shit, and nothing gets discussed unless I'm in the room."

"Then I guess nothing gets discussed, because after tonight, I don't want to see your ugly face again. And if you don't like that? Enjoy your pig roast. Maybe they'll cut your balls off after you're dead. Maybe not."

If looks could maim, Caleb's head would be rolling on the floor beside his feet. "Did no one ever teach you how to play nice in the sandbox for the greater good?" Miles growls.

Caleb rests his elbows on the table, but I know how he moves; he's primed to grab his gun and empty the chamber. "You raped our mother. It's taking every fiber in my body to not bury you in that sandbox right now." His voice has taken on that dangerous edge that is never good.

"That was business."

"Business?" Caleb hisses.

Merrick, who's sitting beside him, must sense the brewing storm, because he shifts closer, looking ready to pounce, to restrain him.

"Merrick and Vince will work with you," Camillo says.

"But—"

"Enough." He waves away his eldest son's objections, shooting him a warning look.

The muscle in Miles's jaw ticks, his venomous gaze shifting between his youngest brothers, a silent challenge to speak up for him.

Miles will get what he deserves, when the time's right. But here, now, on the top floor of a Vegas high-rise, with Mercy and Michelle above us and the Feds circling below, is not that time.

"We'll be in touch," Vince says coolly, seemingly unperturbed by his oldest brother's lethal stare.

"Good." Camillo nods to Merrick, who retrieves an envelope that's folded and tucked in his dress pants pocket, hidden by a suit jacket. He tosses it onto the table in front of me.

"What's that?"

Camillo taps the paper with his wrinkled index finger. "*You* have an in-house problem you need to deal with before we meet again."

Fuck. He means Moe. Much like they delivered the proof of Uncle Peter's duplicity as a sign of good faith, the Perris are now giving me a heads-up about our mole. How Merrick keeps uncovering this intel is beyond me. I'm starting to think his guy is better than Stanley. I'm sure Camillo is the one who ordered the archeological dig into us before claiming a side of our bed. They haven't lasted this long by taking reckless chances, and the Easton name is already risky, what with my father behind bars and my uncle being a traitorous bastard. It's self-serving on their part—if we're in business together and Moe talks, we all go down—but still, I'm beginning to appreciate having Vince and Merrick on our side.

"Yeah. We know." It's going to be a long, messy night of extracting secrets to find out exactly how badly that fucker has betrayed us.

It's the last thing I want to spend my night doing. I'd rather spend it with Mercy, making sure she knows that she never has to be afraid of me.

It was a punch to the gut, listening to her cop to those little secret meetings, watching her shake in fear. And knowing that she considered turning on me for even a minute? It felt like someone had reached into my chest and seized my heart and was squeezing... squeezing... squeezing.

But she had a chance to free her dad by fucking me over, and she didn't take it, and that says a lot.

I trust her. As much as I trust Caleb. I never thought I'd be able to say that about a woman.

Caleb gives me curious frown. Well, *he* doesn't know about Moe. Yet. *Not now.* I shake my head and collect the envelope, tucking it into my back pocket. Between the hunt for our dear family and sitting across a table from our mother's murderers and not pulling the trigger, Caleb's already a live wire. Knowing about Moe will only send him into a rage. He needs to keep his focus and his cool.

Camillo eases himself out of the chair with a wince. "Let us know when your end is clear." Leo, Merrick, and Vince follow, rounding the table and heading for the door.

Only Miles lingers, as if challenging both Caleb's demand and his father's edict. He doesn't want this alliance. That much is obvious.

"Now!" Camillo barks.

Finally, Miles hauls his girth out of his seat, but he does so at a leisurely pace. Caleb and I stand with him, not trusting him to loom over us. "Sorry. Just got caught *reminiscing*." The wicked smile that curls his lips sets me on edge.

He's baiting my brother, testing how far he can push him before Caleb blows. Everyone knows Caleb has a temper.

I knew this meeting was a bad idea.

"Caleb...," I warn.

"That dinner tonight wasn't satisfying. I could use something hearty." Caleb smacks his lips like an obnoxious prick. "Like a plate of some good old-fashioned handmade gnocchi. Anyone have a good hookup for me?"

The air in the room shifts, electrifying like it does just before a storm.

My palm twitches, itching to reach for my gun.

"You know what? I was wrong." Miles's sights are set on my brother. "It wasn't business. That was *all* pleasure."

Miles doesn't even have the chance to take aim with his gun before Caleb fires two shots into his chest, followed swiftly by a single bullet to Leo's temple. It's executed without so much as a flinch, as if planned ahead of time.

They're dead before they hit the marble floor, and then Caleb turns his gun on Camillo.

"Cale!" I shout, but what's the point? He's committed us to at least three bodies now. All I can do now is hope the music from the club will drown out the sound of the shots fired.

"It was him or us," he says calmly, aiming the barrel at the old man's forehead.

Camillo hasn't made an attempt to reach for a weapon. The stone-cold fucker's face barely twitches as his gaze shifts between his two dead sons on the floor and the two standing there, doing nothing as their brothers are gunned down. Do they feel an urge to defend their father? As hateful as mine is, I would have a hard time standing by and watching someone attempt to kill him.

I see the stark realization in Camillo's snakish eyes. It's one I'm sure I'll remember until my last breath. The moment where Camillo realizes that everything he has spent his lifetime building is about to come crashing down, thanks in part to his own flesh and blood, and there's nothing he can do.

That understanding is followed by resignation. "I didn't think you had it in you," he says simply.

"Two decades of pent-up hatred and anger for the men who raped and murdered our mother? Oh, believe me. It's *never* gone away," Caleb pushed out through gritted teeth.

"Was this the plan all along? Bring us here and execute us? Right under the Feds' noses? That doesn't seem smart."

Fuck. Moe.

"Pretending to go into business with you is what was stupid." Caleb takes a step in. "This *alliance* never would have worked. You would have fucked us over the first chance you got."

"Yes," Camillo admits without a hint of shame. "Miles struggled to see the endgame. Vlad's behind bars; his henchman will find Peter and his sons sooner or later. You two don't have what it takes to survive in this world. It would be a waste to let it all fall into your hands. Though... it seems you were smart enough to make other alliances all on your own." His gaze shifts to his remaining sons, who stand quietly as they watch their family being gunned down, tension radiating from their bodies.

Is that a father's pain or pride that I see in his eyes?

"We'll take care of mom," Vince offers, his voice strained, his jaw clenching.

Camillo nods once before regarding his youngest son. "I thought you'd be the one to kill Miles after what he did to your *friend*, but I should have known. You always were too soft for this life. What a disappointment."

Merrick's jaw drops in a moment of shock. "You knew about Ryan?"

"Of course I knew." Camillo lets out soft, slow sigh. It's followed by an oddly peaceful smile. "Who do you think told Miles to kill him?"

It takes Merrick a second to process what his father is saying, and another to raise his gun, point, and fire a bullet between the man's eyes.

Camillo Perri crumples to the floor.

And a woman's shrill scream echoes through the penthouse.

SEVENTEEN
MERCY

We trail Moe into the in-suite penthouse elevator, Michelle's massive hot pink suitcase in his grip. He may be an FBI informant and part of a hit squad for a crime family, but he's all those things with gentlemanly manners, insisting on collecting the hefty luggage for her.

"I think you should stay the night. Please? You can leave in the morning. You've had too much to drink." She's been drinking since we arrived at noon, and that last martini that Moe brought and she chugged was especially potent. "You can stay in my room with me."

She offers me a weak smile. "Yeah, I'll bet Gabriel would love that."

"He probably would." My joke is delivered with a matching weak laugh. "We can get you another room. We *are* in a hotel. I'm sure there are a few available."

We step out of elevator and into the main room just as the heavy pocket doors to the games room slide open. Inside, men are standing and shuffling around the poker table. Men who murdered Gabriel and Caleb's mother. I'm instantly on edge.

"...wasn't business. That was all pleasure," says an unfamiliar gruff voice.

A commotion stirs, with shouts and warnings.

I jolt with the first loud bang. It's followed closely by a second and then a third.

A wave of shock slams into me as Farley and bodyguard named Max swarm the open door, their guns drawn, and Gabriel shouts his brother's name.

"Get back upstairs!" Moe barks at us, abandoning the suitcase and drawing his gun.

But Michelle and I are frozen in place. We can't see into the room, the half-drawn doors successfully blocking whatever horror awaits. Was Caleb just shot? Is he dead?

No, I think that's him I hear talking. I can't make out what he's saying over the pounding blood in my ears, but I recognize that cadence.

Another shot fires, and a gray-haired man drops to the floor in the doorway, his lifeless gaze settled on us. In seconds, a trickle of blood leaks from the hole between his eyes, down along his nose, to pool on the marble tile.

Beside me, Michelle lets out a bloodcurdling scream.

Me? I can't seem to find my voice.

The pocket door flies open, and Gabriel steps out. "What the *hell* are they doing down here?" he roars, his eyes wild with panic.

"Michelle wanted to leave," Moe explains calmly. Meanwhile, his gun is trained on Merrick and Vince.

"They're fine. Lower your weapons." Caleb is alive and well and frowning at the floor in the room. Now that the doors are wide open, I see two other lifeless bodies lying there.

My heart feels like it's going to leap from my chest.

Gabriel shifts his focus away from us for the moment. "This is not what we planned!"

"Maybe not, but the end result is the same." Caleb nudges one of the men's shoes with his foot. "*Mostly* the same."

Gabriel pushes his hand through his hair as he surveys the bloody mess.

"I told Dad this was a bad idea, right from the start," Caleb says.

"Well, good. You can tell him that again, every day, when we're sharing a goddamn cell with him. How the hell are we going to clean this up!" I've never seen Gabriel so unnerved.

His words seem to spur everyone into action.

Caleb snaps his fingers at Farley. "See if anyone heard those shots. We need to know how fast we have to move."

The big man nods and ducks his head to begin chattering into his earpiece.

"I know a cleaner. Excellent in these kinds of situations," the younger blond man—Merrick, I think, though we've never been properly introduced—stands over the old man's body, peering down at him, his gun still clutched in his hand. His voice sounds hollow. Is he the one who fired that last shot?

How many times have they been in these sorts of situations, to deem someone "excellent"?

I watch in a surreal fog as everyone sets into action to cover up a triple murder.

Beside me, Michelle trembles. "I can't believe this is happening," she whispers, tears streaming down her cheeks.

"Get them away from here," Caleb orders. It takes me a moment to realize he's talking about us.

Moe nods, reaches for the suitcase.

"Not you." Gabriel aims his gun at the bodyguard, and everyone in the room stops moving, along with my heart.

My thoughts echo Michelle's words: *Is this really happening?*

Oh God. Moe may unsettle me, but I don't want to see this. I don't want to see Gabriel kill him. I don't want to see Gabriel as a murderer. I want to keep wearing my blinders.

Moe slowly pulls his hand away from the luggage.

"Back away from him, Mercy. Now," Gabriel demands in a harsh voice that doesn't sound like him, easing in closer, his eyes never leaving the man.

I grab Michelle's arm and herd her toward the elevator doors. I would drag her all the way upstairs if we could get past Moe without risking becoming a hostage, because that's the only way Moe is getting out of this situation alive.

"Gabe?" Caleb watches his brother intently. "What the fuck is going on?"

"Stanley got a heads-up that the Feds have an informant here."

Moe slowly raises arms in the air. He doesn't even attempt to pull out his gun. "I'm not the rat." He doesn't sound surprised by the accusation, though.

"So you're denying it? Are you saying that you didn't stand watch while that fucking agent cornered Mercy and threatened her?"

Caleb's gaze flash to mine, his eyebrows raised in question.

I push past the mind-numbing fear that has seized me and manage the slightest nod.

A hint of concern furrows his brow. It's a rare sight, and I don't know if it's concern for me or himself, but it's nice to see, all the same.

"Yeah, there was an agent in the restroom tonight, rattling her," Moe admits calmly.

"And earlier, at the spa."

Moe's brow furrows. "I didn't know about that one."

"Bullshit. You brought her back because you were hoping to find something like *this* mess." Gabriel aims the gun at Moe's forehead. His finger hovers over the trigger. He looks seconds away from pulling it.

I wince, bracing myself.

"It's not him," Merrick calls out, stalling Gabriel's itchy finger.

Moe's eyes flicker between the two men before settling on Gabriel. "I brought Mercy back because they insisted, and because I thought she might be feeding the Feds information on you. I thought you'd want to deal with it. But it's not her." Moe releases a reluctant sigh. "It's the other one."

I frown. *The other one*? What does he mean by "the other one"?

Not until Moe turns to study Michelle does it click.

"Are you insane? She's not an FBI *informant!*" It's almost laughable.

That is, until Michelle starts to cry uncontrollably, a barely coherent "I'm sorry" slipping from her lips.

Icy dread slips down my spine as what she's saying registers. "Oh my God, Michelle, *what did you do*?"

"My father... She said they'd drop the charges...." Her words break apart with her sobs.

"What the fuck." Caleb studies the woman he's been flirting with and bedding for the past few days as if she's suddenly grown tentacles on her forehead and revealed herself in alien form.

Gabriel frowns as if trying to figure out a complex problem. His gun is still in hand, though lowered. I can't even guess at what's going through his mind right now. What I do know is that he was about to shoot Moe for being an informant.

Michelle just admitted to being an informant.

If he hurts her...

I do the only thing I can think of.

I step in front my best friend, shielding her from harm as I silently plead with those dark and stormy eyes for mercy.

EIGHTEEN
GABRIEL

"No reports of gunfire yet," Farley confirms.

Caleb's head falls back with his heavy relief. "Okay. Get working on the security system. We're going to need some camera interference to pull this off. And I want the feed from the parking garage and the service elevator destroyed. Get details on all the guards."

Farley nods and ambles off.

"It's all gone to shit. Perris are dead, Peter is in hiding. The Feds are crawling up our asses. We have a fucking informant." Caleb begins to pace. "*This* is why we don't ever get involved with women. *This* is why we fuck and then they leave, and that's the end of it. I told you we shouldn't have brought them here!"

"They don't know anything."

He stops abruptly to glare at me. "You mean besides the three dead bodies? They're both goddamn witnesses!"

"Because *you* couldn't control yourself! You just couldn't wait until the timing was right." I sigh. Getting in a screaming match won't do anyone any good. "Mercy's not going to talk. She's smart, and she wants to protect her father." And she's in love with me.

At least I hope she's *still* in love with me after seeing that side of me.

My gaze shifts to the terrace, to where Mercy and Michelle sit huddled on the sectional couch, Terrence watching over them. I couldn't get a read on Mercy other than to know that she's terrified. Is she mad at her best friend? Feeling betrayed? Her initial shock wasn't enough to stop her from jumping in front of Michelle to protect her from us. That was some brave shit, but I shouldn't be surprised.

"Yeah? What about the other one, huh? The one that's already sitting nicely in the Feds' pocket? What the fuck are we going to do about *her*?"

"Maybe if you'd kept your dick out of America for two minutes, she wouldn't be so eager to crucify you," I mutter.

"Give me a break. She was already talking to them before that. She was screwing me while trying to fuck me."

"She had nothing to tell them. She doesn't know shit." Because Mercy doesn't know shit. Nothing that could be used as a smoking gun against us, anyway.

Caleb shakes his head. He's not convinced. "They've had that coming for twenty years. We are *not* getting buried for that." He stabs a finger toward the games room.

He's angry, I get it. If this were Moe or Vic or any other backstabbing two-faced prick, we'd be talking about how deep a hole we need to bury that secret. But even we have limits, and ending a woman who witnessed something she shouldn't have because we were sloppy is not an option.

"We need to get more details. Find out exactly what she's told them so far."

"And then what?" Caleb pushes. "Sit back and hope she doesn't crack under pressure? Fucking look at her!"

"Yeah, she's a terrified mess." The woman broke down in a hysterical fit the second Moe outed her. It's no wonder this agent was able to coerce her into complying. Who knows what they have on her family, but it'd take nothing to sway her. That works to our advantage. I grit my teeth. This is the part of this dirty business that I hate most. "So we make sure she understands what happens to her and her loved ones if she says a word about this to anyone." Strike the kind of fear in her that shuts her down.

And hope Mercy doesn't hate me for it.

Merrick ends his call with this mystery cleaner then. "He's on his way," he announces, downing a shot of whatever clear booze Vince just poured him.

I'll give it to these two—they have connections. "You told him to use the service elevator?"

"He knows. It's not the first time he's been here." Merrick sounds robotic. They're both stone-faced and operating in strict get-shit-done mode. I can't blame them, seeing as they just watched three family members get gunned down, one by their own hands. Certainly not how we expected tonight to go. "He's not cheap, especially given circumstances. How much cash do you guys have on you?"

"We'll have to check the safe, but enough." Caleb never comes to Sin City without a few hundred thousand to gamble away.

"He wants payment upfront." Merrick dumps another shot down his gullet.

"Hey, you want to ease up on that before you get railed and blow this for all of us?" Caleb warns.

I glare at my brother. *Pot. Kettle.* And so not the time to be scolding the man. He just put a bullet in his father's head. Even *I* don't have the stomach to do that, and I hate the bastard. I wouldn't have thought Merrick had the stomach either, but I guess finding out that your father hired a hit on someone you love does strange things to people.

"No, I don't fucking want to ease up," Merrick snarls, turning on my brother, his hands twitching by his sides like they're craving a weapon to fire or a face to smash. "There wouldn't be anything to *blow* if you had just kept your big mouth shut."

"Are you *seriously* trying to pin this on me?" Caleb's shoulders stiffen. "You were here! He was going to kill us!"

"Yeah. Because you kept poking him. You knew where that would lead!"

"You know what? Why are you so fucking angry? You guys are free! We just solved *all* your problems and then some. No more dirty drug business. Merrick, you can fly your flag and suck all the cock—"

Merrick lunges.

Vince jumps in between them, grabbing hold of his brother and wrestling him away. "Enough! There'll be plenty of time later for you two to beat the shit out of each other. Let's focus on the task at hand." He waits until Merrick nods before releasing his grip. "We took the service elevator up, so the Feds might know we were meeting here tonight, but hopefully they don't have an exact headcount."

Caleb adopts a casual stance, his arms folded across his chest. "'Hopefully' is a gamble I'm not willing to take."

"That's why we wipe all evidence that that were here. But they can't just disappear off the map without a trace. That just guarantees that the Feds are up our asses for years, especially since they've already been seen around Vegas. And those two?" He points to Mercy and Michelle. "They'll eventually crack under that kind of pressure."

"So what are you suggesting?" I ask.

"They need to find the bodies."

"You're talking about staging it."

"Yeah."

That makes this entire cleanup process way more complicated. And expensive. But also probably smart. "You've got any ideas?"

"I do." Vince's jaw tenses. "I think it's time to make use of this turf war with Navarro."

Point the Feds toward the cartel. Definitely smart, if we can pull it off. "Okay. I'll find out what I can from the ladies. You guys decide how we're going to roll." I head for the terrace, throwing over my shoulder, "And if you're gonna kill each other, do it before the cleaner gets here so he can throw your bodies in with the others."

I probably shouldn't joke.

NINETEEN
MERCY

"My parents have been having money issues over the past couple of years. I guess it got *really* bad, because my dad took out some bank loans. You know, to keep up appearances and lifestyle and all that. And to make sure he got what he needed, he fudged the store numbers." Michelle blows her nose on a tissue and then balls it up to toss it onto the small mountain of others. After fifteen minutes of hysterical sobbing where she couldn't string a sentence together, she has finally calmed down enough to explain herself. "They caught him and charged him with bank fraud."

I can't help my gasp. Mr. Banks always seemed like an honest, upstanding citizen. "When did this happen?"

"They arrested him about three weeks ago."

Three weeks? "Why didn't you tell me!" And how hadn't I heard about it?

"Because I'm mortified! We all are. We'll probably lose the store. My mom is talking about leaving him."

Despite the burn of betrayal, my heart aches for her. "Yeah, but I'm your best friend. We've been through so much together. You didn't trust me?" She was my sounding board through the dark days after Fleet's attack on me and my father's arrest and conviction.

"I figured you had enough on your plate with your father and... other things." Her green, mascara-streaked eyes dart to Gabriel, who just emerged from inside and now hovers over the terrace sectional like a sentry, his arms folded across his powerful chest. He hastily tucked his gun away the moment I stepped in front of Michelle. I assume that was a signal that he had no intention of harming her—or at least not yet.

He wouldn't.

Would he?

Despite the warm, dry desert air, Michelle clutches her blanket as though it's the dead of winter in the arctic. Sitting out here, with the muted sounds of Vegas's bustling nightlife carrying from far below, one could almost forget that inside there are three dead bodies tucked behind the pocket doors.

Almost.

"When did they approach you?" Gabriel asks.

She bites her lip, hesitant to respond. "The day after Caleb drove me home from Empire."

"That was a week ago!" Michelle's been conspiring with the FBI for a whole week? Is that why she was pushing to hook up with Caleb? And why she came to Vegas to celebrate? And why she stuck close to me last night?

I pick through my memories, thinking back to *all* my conversations with her over the past three weeks. Frankly there weren't that many, and when we did talk, it was usually about Gabriel or my father or my upcoming exams. It was always about *my* life, my problems.

"They must have had a tail on us that night," Gabriel says.

"But why go after *Michelle*? Why not me?"

"Because they weren't sure if they could flip you on their own. They found leverage they could use on her, and she's a stepping-stone to get to you." He's so matter-of-fact about it.

"Seems like a lot of work."

His responding chuckle is sinister. "Babe, you wouldn't believe the lengths they'll go to. They've probably been digging for dirt on you for weeks."

Before last night's explosion, then.

"They knew who you were," Michelle confirms. "Lewis showed up at my condo and started asking all kinds of questions."

Dread slides down my spine. I don't want to be a part of any investigation. "About?"

"Everything. About your mom, your dad, about Gabriel. She wanted to know how you guys met."

Oh, God. "And what did you tell them!"

She winces. "The truth? Sort of?"

My stomach twists. No wonder Lewis knew so much. She wasn't guessing. She'd already mined private information from my best friend, who knew about the deal Gabriel offered me. Hell, she and I even sat at the coffee shop and mapped out my list of demands for staying longer. Is there a document somewhere that outlines exactly how Gabriel bought me?

A thought strikes me, and I panic. "Did you tell them about the money for my dad's appeal?"

"No! I didn't tell her about that." She shakes her head furtively. "I swear."

Still... "How *could* you?"

A fresh wave of tears erupts. "I'm sorry! I freaked out!"

Her words give me pause. I said the same thing to Gabriel earlier today when he asked me why I hadn't told him about Lewis ambushing me right away.

That woman is intimidating, I'll give her that.

"What did they promise you?" Gabriel is far more calm than I expected him to be.

Michelle takes a moment to collect herself. "She told me that she could make all the charges against my dad go away if I would tell her everything I knew, and if I helped convince Mercy to work with her."

"And you agreed?" I can't help the accusation in my tone. "I can't believe you would do something like that."

"I didn't know you—" She stops abruptly, as if guarding her words. "I didn't know how you felt about him. And I thought, given what you'd *already* agreed to for your father, that this wouldn't be a big deal."

"Informing on a crime family to put them away. Yeah. Not a big deal at all." I shake my head at my best friend, my tone harsh.

"I'm sorry," she whines. "I didn't know what else to do! My dad can't go to jail! I've seen what's happening to your dad, and it's horrible."

"But it's okay to help send us there." I hadn't noticed Caleb come outside. He settles onto the arm of the couch closest to Michelle. It's a casual pose, and yet the way he looms over her, the way he stares down at her, is menacing. All traces of their playfulness have vanished.

Michelle shrinks in her seat.

"What *exactly* have you told them? We need to know everything," Gabriel pushes, steering the conversation back to the FBI. "How you communicated, how often, *everything*."

"Umm... sure. Yeah, okay." She swallows hard. "By text, usually. Sometimes she calls."

"On this phone?" Caleb slides the phone he confiscated from her out of his pocket.

She nods.

He holds the phone out. "Show me the messages."

"I don't have any. I delete them right away. She told me to." Michelle stumbles over her words.

"When did you last communicate?" Caleb fires off questions as if by script, his demeanor cool.

She hesitates, her eyes flashing to mine. "When I was upstairs with Mercy. I went to the bathroom and I texted to tell her that you guys knew someone was talking to the FBI. I told her I was afraid, and I was renting a car and leaving tonight." Her voice shakes.

Jesus. And there I was, warning her against mentioning Gabriel and Caleb's illicit activities because of Moe, talking about how they were going to kill him because he was working with the Feds. No wonder all the blood drained from her face.

"Shit!"

Caleb's sharp curse makes Michelle and me jump.

"Why?" I look to Gabriel. "What does it matter if they know that you know?"

Gabriel exchanges an unreadable look with Caleb. "It's just better when we have the upper hand, is all."

"Did you tell her who was here?" Caleb's calm mask is slipping, his voice more frantic.

"I said there were a bunch of men—"

"How many?" He barks and she jumps.

"I didn't say. I just recognized the two from the club last week, but I didn't recognize the others."

He sighs heavily.

Michelle's phone chirps then, as if on cue.

Caleb reads the screen. "Lux Nails."

"That's her. She's probably checking on me. I should have been downstairs by now."

"I guess we need to answer her then." Caleb hands Michelle her phone. "Open it."

She hands it back to him with a trembling grip.

"Texting to confirm that you're keeping your appointment?" He grunts. "Clever. Are there any code words you use? Anything to verify that it's you responding?"

She shakes her head.

"If you're lying—"

"I'm not! I swear!" she stammers. "She said this was safe, that you'd never find out."

"So she lied to you *and* put you in danger. Big surprise." His thumbs fly over the screen. "Okay, you've just told her that you've changed your mind about leaving. You've had too much to drink and you don't want to leave Mercy in the frazzled state she's in. They're pretty sure the informant was either Felix or Finn." The muscle in Caleb's jaw ticks. He doesn't like using his dead friends as scapegoats. "Let's hope they buy that, for your sake, because if they bust in here right now, it's going to get very bloody, very fast."

"Am I...." She swallows and asks in a barely audible whisper, "Are you going to hurt me?"

"For what? Fucking me while working with a federal agent to try and send us to prison?" His voice is emotionless as he watches the screen for a reply. Is he angry? Hurt? Feeling foolish? "You know, those guys lying in there? The three dead guys?"

Her eyes flash to the glass doors that lead inside, though she can't see them. She nods.

"If you did to them what you did to us, you wouldn't be

sitting on this couch, having a conversation right now. They would have taken turns raping you and then sunk a bullet into your head and left you in a ditch. Just like they did to our mother."

She lets out a horrified sob.

"Oh, look. A response." He pauses to read. "Agent Bitch has asked what 'they're' up to. I guess that's us, right? She wants to know if we're committing any crimes you can tell her about?" He snorts as he types a response. "See how concerned she is about your well-being?"

Farley pokes his head out of the door to announce, "He's here."

Behind him, I catch a glimpse of a short, bald man in blue coveralls carrying a black case with him into the games room. There's nothing remarkable or threatening about him. He looks like any average man walking down the street. But this must be this "cleaner," here to erase all traces of the bodies.

Behind him, Moe wheels in a housekeeping laundry bin.

I still can't believe this is happening and I'm a witness to it.

Caleb slides down to take a seat on the couch next to Michelle. He stretches his arm across the back, behind her. "So, here's what's going to happen, Michelle. You're going to give me your password, and I'm going to keep your phone for the night to make sure this agent doesn't find cause to come looking for you. We're going to go deal with this little problem of ours, and then we're going to continue on like nothing happened. You're going to get really drunk, so it's hard to keep track of details." His hand settles on her bare knee. "We're going to keep you nice and close for the rest of this trip. And then, when we're back in Phoenix, the next time this agent comes at you, you're going to tell her you saw nothing out of the ordinary and that Mercy doesn't know anything either, but she'll *never* flip on Gabriel. Because she's loyal, and she's not stupid." He pauses and when he speaks again, his tone has taken on a dangerous edge. "There is nothing we can't find out and nowhere out of our reach. If you so much as breathe another word about us to this agent or any other law enforcement, we will find out about it." He leans in to whisper something in her ear.

A fresh wave of tears stream down her cheeks. Whatever he's saying to her, it's scaring her.

He finally pulls away. "You understand me, right?"

Her head bobs furtively as she swallows hard. She looks ready to vomit. I feel the spasm of sympathy deep in the pit of my stomach for her, but it's diluted by shock and the sting of her disloyalty.

"Good girl." Caleb gives her knee an affectionate pat before he stands. "You ladies get yourselves a drink or two. It's going to be a long night."

Gabriel leans in, clasping my chin within gentle fingers to lift my gaze to his. That wild darkness in his eyes has faded. Now, I see nothing but worry and fatigue. "You good?"

I don't know what I am, but I nod anyway. I want to ask him so many questions, and at the same time, I don't want to know anything about what transpired. Seeing the dead bodies was explanation enough.

"Okay. Let's just get through this next bit and then we can figure out the rest."

Figure out the rest of *what*? Of *us*? Is there an "us" after this mess?

He seems unnerved, at least. Cold-blooded murderers

who kill regularly likely aren't concerned by what they've done. That brings me some small comfort.

He moves to follow his brother into the house.

"I'm so sorry—" Michelle begins, but I cut her off.

"Does your dad know about this arrangement you've made with the Feds?"

"My dad?" She shakes her head. "God, no. He'd never be okay with me risking my life for him."

The deep ache of sadness and disappointment pierces my chest. She was trying to save her father from incarceration. I understand that part, more than anyone. "But you were willing to risk *my* life." That's the glaring issue.

Her mouth opens, but she falters, several times over, searching for the right response to that. Is there a right response? "You said you didn't think he'd hurt you."

Whether I believe Gabriel would harm me or not doesn't matter. What matters is that Michelle believes he would. Earlier, she argued that I was being naïve for thinking otherwise. Yet, she still went ahead with helping that FBI agent to corner, coax, and threaten me, to try and convince me to turn on Gabriel.

Michelle has been my best friend and confidante for years, and yet just like that, all trust between us has been destroyed. I don't know how I'll ever see her the same way again.

I could ease her fears now. I could tell her that I still believe that. I could tell her that, if they were going to kill us for what we saw, they would have done it already. After all, what's two more dead bodies to the mix?

But in that moment, my hurt overpowers my compassion. "They'll kill you and your family. Your father, you mother, Lisa..., Bo. All of them. If you ever say a word about tonight to anyone, they *will* find out." My legs feel wobbly as I stand and calmly walk to the poolside bar to fix us drinks, her sobs drowned out by the sounds of the city below.

The bedroom door creaks open, and the sound of drunken feminine laughter slips into the dimly lit room.

I break from my quiet observation of the terrace—the half that can be seen from our suite—to peer over my shoulder. My heart stutters at the sight of Gabriel. Even in the low cast of the bedside lamp, the dark circles beneath his eyes are visible. It's after 4:00 a.m. and he has slept for maybe three hours in the last thirty. "You look exhausted."

He tosses his watch and phone on the nightstand. His gun, he sets down more carefully. I'm already getting used to seeing him with it. "Moe said you came up here an hour ago. I thought you'd already be asleep." His voice is croaky, like it sounds in the moments after he first wakes up.

"So did I." But I can't quiet my mind, I can't ease this guilt that weighs on me, that Gabriel might feel betrayed by me, as I do by Michelle. "I'm sorry. I should have told you about Lewis right away."

He sighs heavily. "I know you are."

Is he still upset with me though?

I turn back to the view of the pool, afraid of what comes next for us. Blackmail... betrayal... murder... Was there ever any hope for a real, normal relationship between us?

A light switch clicks, and the room is thrown into darkness. Footfalls approach from behind me. His hands settle on my hips, smoothing over them in a soothing manner.

"How's the hotel thing going?" I nod toward Caleb, who's been talking to Bruce Cohen by the bar for the past half hour. It seems to be a friendly conversation. I wonder if this guy will be as friendly toward Caleb when the FBI shows up with a warrant and a forensics team to dissect this place, looking for evidence. Does he realize who Mr. Green *really* is?

"Not great, but Caleb's determined. He's trying to find out who his business partners are. Bruce owns a majority stake, but he has partners who can be pressed, if needed."

"So he doesn't want to sell, is that what you're saying?"

"Everyone has a price." His lips are tender as they move to the crook of my neck, and I tip my head to the side, reveling in it. He pulls my body into his, and I feel the tension coursing through his body. He's far from at ease.

Silence hangs in our darkened bedroom, as I search for what to say next.

My gaze drifts to the sectional couch, where Michelle is curled up, asleep, and the now familiar mix of hurt, anger, and sympathy stirs. I haven't talked to her since I left her on the couch. She quietly disappeared into the powder room to clean herself up, reemerging just as Gabriel and Caleb came to collect us.

The four of us, plus Merrick and Vince, Farley and Moe, bounced from club to club, skating past lines and door lists, staying just long enough to make our presence known and keep any FBI tails on us distracted. True to Gabriel's promise, Farley stuck so close to Michelle all night, his body heat must have kept her warm. She said nothing to anyone, accepting drinks and smiling politely.

It was after two when we arrived back at the penthouse to a small horde of mostly women on the terrace. The cleaner—and the bodies—were already long gone, leaving not a trace of evidence, not even a hint of bleach in the air.

The morbid side of me wonders what they used to erase the murders.

Michelle bypassed the skinny-dippers without so much as a glance and curled up in a corner of the sectional, visibly exhausted. At some point Merrick settled next to her and gently coaxed her down to rest her head on his lap, covering her with her blanket. He didn't seem in much of a mood for a party either. Not like his brother, who had a scantily clad woman rubbing up against his thigh before disappearing with her.

"She's safe there, right? He seems decent but..." He's a Perri.

"She's safe there." Gabriel rests his chin on my shoulder.

The question that's been burning my tongue for hours slips free. "What happened tonight?"

"Things didn't go as planned."

No shit. They clearly hadn't planned on ending their meeting with three dead bodies in our penthouse. I hesitate. "Did you... Were any of those bullets fired from your gun?"

"Is that your polite way of asking me if I killed anyone?"

"I guess."

"No. I didn't."

A weight lifts from my chest. He must have felt it, too.

"Do you want to hear about it?"

Do I? The fact that Gabriel's offering to tell me doesn't go unnoticed. It means he trusts me more today than he did yesterday, even though I'm being pressed by Agent Lewis.

My chest swells with that knowledge as I nod.

"Miles Perri was as much of a hothead as Caleb is, and he was looking for an excuse to kill him. He brought up our mother, they went back and forth a bit, and then Miles drew his gun. Luckily Caleb was faster."

"You both could have died tonight."

"Yeah. It's been a busy thirty-six hours. That's two near deaths." His tone is full of amusement, but there's nothing funny about that.

I reach for Gabriel's hands, guiding them around me until he's holding me in his arms. "And the others?"

"Leo and Miles are a package deal."

"And the old man?"

"Caleb was going to take him out too, but Merrick did it before he had a chance."

My mouth drops as I study the handsome man who must be around Gabriel's age, his head falling back against the couch. He appears to be asleep. "He shot his own father?"

"Yeah. But his own father had his boyfriend murdered. A guy who had nothing to do with this world. Like you."

"Holy shit." Talk about messed-up family dynamics. "Is he upset?"

"He definitely doesn't seem like himself, but he'll get over it. It's not like it wasn't coming. It just wasn't supposed to happen tonight. And Leo wasn't a part of the plan. He didn't give a shit about family legacy. He'd be happy to cut out the others to run it himself. Like my uncle and cousins."

"And Merrick and Vince are okay with that?"

"They want out as much as we do. Now, they'll probably take over the family's wineries and venture into a few other businesses. Legit ones."

Pieces are starting to fit together. "So, this whole plan to get away from the drug business, *those* two have been in on it all along?"

"Yeah. And the only way that's going to happen is if our family is dealt with."

Dealt with. As in dead.

"But your father is still alive."

"For now."

A shiver skitters through my body. That sounds like a promise. I tell myself that I don't want to know what they have planned. It's called plausible deniability, and I need to wade deep in that pond, given I have Lewis hounding me.

At least the terrace is quickly emptying of people. Only a few stragglers linger by the bar, pouring back shots that they'll feel tomorrow.

I watch as Moe's sleek form closes in on where Michelle and Merrick doze. Only, Merrick's head snaps up as if on guard. Words are exchanged and then Moe collects Michelle's sleeping body with slow, gentle movements, like a parent would pick up their child.

"Moe will carry her to bed," Gabriel says, answering the question before I have a chance to ask.

"Whose bed. Caleb's?" Talk about a living nightmare. As if tonight wasn't bad enough. She shouldn't have to wake up next to the man.

Gabriel chuckles and points to where two women—one the blond showgirl who rode his lap earlier—have peeled off their costumes and are stepping into the pool naked, each beckoning him with crooked fingers. "Caleb's not going to sleep tonight."

I can see his mischievous grin from here as he begins shedding clothes. I shake my head. It's a good thing Michelle is unconscious. "Is this what normally happens when you guys come to Vegas? Booze and debauchery?"

"And excessive gambling. Usually no dead bodies."

I turn to give him a flat look.

"This is pretty tame," he admits, his eyes twinkling.

I shift my focus back to Moe—I don't want to think about the kinds of things Gabriel has done with other women while here—and watch him whisk Michelle away. My guilt flares. "Is he upset with me?" He didn't say a word to me the entire night, not that he was much of a talker to begin with. But will I be dealing with a bodyguard carrying a grudge from now on?

"No, he gets it."

"I almost got him killed."

"You were trying to protect me. And what were we supposed to think? He *did* ask Farley to be on your detail."

"Yeah. *Why*?" That still doesn't add up.

"From what Farley told me, he has a soft spot for women and children. He likes protecting innocent people, and he's good at it."

And the Eastons are far from innocent. Though, I'm not sure I fit neatly under that label anymore, either.

I turn back just as Caleb strolls into the pool, naked and proud and fully erect. If I didn't know him, it might be an enticing sight. The problem is, I do know him. "I've seen your brother naked far too many times."

Gabriel's dark chuckles tickles my eardrum. "He would argue not enough."

The drunken people by the bar must notice what's happening in the pool then, because they suddenly flock to it in chorus of laughter, stumbling over their feet as they discard their clothes. In less than a minute, there are six drunk naked people in the pool.

Against my back, I feel Gabriel harden. I'm not surprised that he would respond to this free-spirited fuck-fest unfolding below us. Even I'm having a hard time ignoring the heady feeling growing in the air, an intoxicating carelessness that distracts from all our looming worries.

But, the worries are still there.

"So, what now?" I ask softly.

"Now, we enjoy being alive another day while we wait to see how this all plays out tomorrow." Gabriel releases me from his grip to slip his hands beneath my dress. Hooking his fingers in the sides of my panties, he slides them off. They fall to the floor, settling on my heels.

I gasp as his finger slides into me from behind. "Gabriel—"

"Relax. It's dark in here, and no one cares anyway."

He's probably right, I realize, watching as the two women swarm Caleb, each pressing up to a side of him, taking turns kissing him, their hands disappearing beneath the water to tag team a hand job. The other three—two men and a woman—have grouped off, settling onto the steps, three sets of hands wandering over flesh with curious abandon. Only Merrick sits on the couch, a glass of something in his grip, quietly watching the spectacle.

"You know that I could never hurt you, right? Even if you had taken that agent's deal... " His words drift. "I haven't been a good man, Mercy. Not to you, not to anyone. I probably deserve to rot in a cell for the rest of my life."

My breathing is turning ragged beneath his touch. "That's not what I want."

"What *do* you want then?"

"You. Just you." I widen my stance to give him better access.

He takes it, sinking two more fingers deep inside me, hitting that spot with deft skill. "If you give me a chance, I *will* change."

All I can muster is a sound of agreement, as my body betrays my conscience and burns with need.

In the pool below us, Caleb sits perched on the concrete side, his legs splayed wide, allowing his two female companions space to nestle between his thighs. His hands cradle the backs of their heads as he guides their mouths over his dick. But his focus doesn't seem to be on either of them. It's not even up here.

I frown. "Why does Caleb look like he's staring at Merrick?"

"Because he's probably taunting him, like the narcissistic asshole that he is." Gabriel's teeth graze my earlobe, and hints of his normal playfulness emerge. "I need you now."

A flutter stirs in my belly. "I know." And I'll never tire of hearing him say it.

"Do you trust me?"

"Yes." I don't even miss a beat.

With my body, implicitly.

But also with my heart.

Gabriel has my heart, whether or not I want to give it to him.

"What I want, *whenever* I want it. Remember?"

I feel his words between my thighs, even as my stomach clenches. The last time he played that card, he produced a plug from his desk drawer. "Are we back to this again?" I attempt a bored tone, but my voice comes out shaky with nerves.

His chuckle is deep and teasing as his hand slips free of me. "Close your eyes," he demands.

I do as asked, my blood racing in my ears.

With gentle hands, Gabriel slowly guides the straps of my skimpy dress off my shoulders. The silky material slides down my form effortlessly, to pool at my feet. "Keep them closed," he warns, unfastening my strapless bra and tossing it away. "Here. Let me help you," he coaxes, gripping my hips.

With a hard swallow, I lift one heel free from my discarded dress, then the other, acutely aware that I'm standing in a floor-to-ceiling window wearing nothing but these silver five-inch heels. For once, though, I don't feel the need to remind Gabriel that I'm not into his kind of weird kink. Maybe it's the insanity of the past thirty-six hours, maybe it's shock, maybe it's the countless martinis that I've consumed, but right now, nothing seems to faze me.

I listen as Gabriel unfastens his belt buckle and wordlessly sheds his clothes. He sidles up behind me again. His bare skin is burning hot against mine. Still, I tremble from nerves.

"Eyes closed," he reminds me, before angling my face toward him with a thumb under my chin. He lays a sweet, sultry kiss against my mouth, the tip of his tongue skating along the seam of my lips, over and over again. His fingers skate across my cheekbone in an affectionate, teasing stroke, before working their way around to weave through my hair. There's no rush, no hint of his exhaustion, no push to pass foreplay for the main event now that we're both undressed.

Ever so slowly, as Gabriel worships my mouth with languid kisses, everything and everyone else fades into the background. My body buzzes with nervous anticipation, even as it begins grow more comfortable in this highly vulnerable situation.

He must sense it, too, because he guides my hands to the windowpane in front of me, gently pressing my palms against the cool glass. With a whisper of, "keep those there," he molds his hands to my body, sliding them down my arms, down my torso, pausing to cup my breasts and tease my hardened nipples for a few beats, before slipping down to smooth over my hips.

"Have I told you how much I like these shoes?" He

murmurs, dragging the tip of his length through my slick folds.

I shudder and angle my hips for him. "No. Why is that?"

"They put you at the perfect height."

I feel the teasing smile curl my lips, even though he can't see it. "For what?"

He answers by sinking into me with a single, hard thrust.

I let my head fall back and a guttural cry escape my lips as he fills me completely.

"Jesus," he hisses. "Do you even know how hot you are?" It's sounds like an accusation.

I answer by arching my back even more, earning another curse from his lips.

His fingers dig into my hip bones as he begins moving at a steady, unhurried pace, and I brace myself against the glass, relishing how my body stretches and welcomes him, how it craves him. With my eyes closed, I realize just how overwhelmingly familiar Gabriel has become to me—his scent, his touch, his voice, his taste. I could find him in a pitch-black room full of bodies, with any of those.

But all of them together?

All the things that make Gabriel Easton who he is?

Heat pools at the apex of my thighs as I allow myself to feel every inch of him. When it comes to my body, he has *never* led me astray. Every time he touches me, I know I'm going to enjoy what he does.

My curiosity replaces my nervousness.

That's when I dare open my eyes and take in the scene below us.

The group of three by the pool stairs are gone. Meanwhile, Caleb and his two women have left the pool and ventured over to the couch, where the blond grinds on Caleb's lap, her enormous breasts swaying. The brunette has turned her affections to Merrick. Her hand is down the front of his pants, moving rhythmically. He's not making any moves to reciprocate or even suggest he cares that she's there, but he's also not pushing her away.

Isn't that sweet... Caleb is sharing a dick-swapper with his sworn enemy.

She leans in and whispers something in Merrick's ear and, after a lengthy moment, he lifts his hips. She wastes no time, yanking his pants and briefs down his powerful thighs, springing his erection free. She eagerly dives in, taking him into her mouth.

That finally gets a reaction of the seemingly despondent man, as Merrick's head falls back against the couch. Even from this distance, I can make out the sharp, sexy jut of his Adam's apple, and the way his lips part in a satisfied moan.

Damn, between the Easton boys and the two youngest Perris, those evil, decrepit crime bosses produced some attractive men.

"Like what you see?" Gabriel says through ragged breaths.

I turn back to spy his devious smile. He caught me watching.

His smile widens. "Don't bother lying to me. You're dripping wet."

My cheeks flush. I *am* dripping wet. "Don't get any ideas. This is a onetime thing." But Gabriel needs it. Maybe *I* need it, too.

"I guess I better make it count then." He shifts his position and, clasping the back of my thigh, he hikes my leg high in the air.

"Gabriel!" I exclaim through nervous laughter, using the window for balance as he displays me for all to see.

His other arm slips around my waist to support me. "You're good. I won't let you fall," he whispers into my ear, his face nuzzled in my hair.

It's all I can do to stay upright as Gabriel's hips move with expert skill, thrusting into me over and over again, the moans he manages to pull from my throat frequent and loud. I *should* be embarrassed, but I no longer care what anyone hears.

And I no longer care what Caleb and Merrick can see.

Now, I watch with depraved fascination as the young Perri fists the brunette's long hair, guiding the quick tempo of her mouth as she sucks him off. His steady, dark gaze isn't on her though.

It's not on me.

It's not even on the woman riding Caleb wild.

It's on Caleb, his head resting on the back of the couch, his lips parted, his beautiful, muscular body tensing with an orgasm.

One that has Merrick's hips suddenly jerking upward, and his focus shifting back to the woman whose mouth he's unloading into.

"Time to come, baby." Gabriel slips his fingers between my legs. He barely touches me though, and my body is hit with wave after wave of intense pleasure, buckling my body until Gabriel is all but holding me up, his own guttural cries a distance sound.

"Wow," he murmurs through his heavy pants, releasing his grip of my thigh. My leg drops down like dead weight, the muscles useless. "Thought you said you weren't an exhibitionist."

"Shut up. They can't see anything, remember?" I scold breathlessly, even as my cheeks flush.

The blond has abandoned Caleb's lap to dive into the pool, leaving him sprawled out on the couch, buck naked, and languidly stroking himself while the brunette takes her turn riding Merrick.

Something tells me they'll be going several more rounds before the desert sun rises for the day.

"Oh, they saw," Gabriel teases, wrapping his arms around my body, enveloping me into his strength. "They saw what's mine, forever. Because I'm *never* letting you go."

There was a time not long ago that hearing Gabriel say that would have set off panic inside me. Where I couldn't get away soon enough.

Now?

I'm eager to know what "forever" might feel like with a man like him.

Still, my stubborn side flares, the one that has come to enjoy battling with him. "I guess you better hope that our monthly negotiations go well for you, then. Because I have a new list of demands."

"A new list, huh?" Grabbing my hips, he spins me around to face him. "Remember, two can play at this game."

I stroll past him, to perch on the edge of the bed. I offer him a saccharine smile. "And yet I'll *always* win."A wicked gleam flashes in his eyes as he charges for me.

He's buried deep inside me before my back hits the mattress.

TWENTY
GABRIEL

I WAKE to someone jostling my shoulder.

"Hey. Gabe. You got to get up."

"Fuck off," I mumble into my pillow. I forgot to lock the door.

"No. Seriously. Wake up. It's almost ten, and shit's going down."

I peel my eyelids open. Caleb is standing over me, shifting from foot to foot. He's already dressed and anxious. "Did you even sleep?"

"A few hours."

"Did the Perris leave?"

"Yup. Come on. We're going to play some poker with Cohen."

I snort. "For what? You think you're going to win his hotel with a royal flush?"

"Shut up and get dressed. *Now*." He's at the door when he adds, "They found the bodies."

My eyes fly open. "When?"

But he's already gone. The bastard knew that would get me moving.

I rub the sleep from my eyes and roll onto my back. Mercy is on her stomach, her silky black hair fanned out over the pillow, still deeply asleep. A sexy angel that I'll never get enough of.

The woman I love with everything I am.

It's a strange thing to admit that, but here I am, wearing-my-heart-on-my-sleeve in love with the woman I once bribed to sleep with me.

I can't wait until the day I can camp out between her legs all day.

Unfortunately, that day is not today.

I settle for a feather-soft kiss against her shoulder. I don't want to wake her, so I slip out and dress quietly, scribbling a quick note for her when she wakes up.

"Mr. Green, Mr. Pink Panther." Sienna strolls up to us in the lobby as we're stepping off the elevator, an iPad tucked under her arm. She spares Farley a wary glance. Next to him, she looks like a child. "How has your stay been so far?"

Caleb grins. "Fucking killer."

"Well, good. Please let me know if you need anything."

His eyes dip down the cleavage of her sexy white blouse. "What time are you off tonight? You should come up and join us."

She offers him a pinched smile that screams, "go fuck yourself." "Mr. Cohen told me to tell you he's in the high roller room, waiting for you."

Caleb watches her stroll off, curiosity gleaming in his eyes. "Ten thousand bucks says she's a minx in the sack."

"Ten thousand says that woman despises you and you *never* find out." My burner phone rings in my pocket.

"I'll find out by tomorrow morning!" he hollers over his shoulder on the way toward the casino door, leaving me to answer.

I don't even bother with a hello. I already know it's Stanley. "Where were they?"

"About an hour southwest on 15."

I linger by one of the water fountains. "And what are the cops saying? Any suspects?"

"Given who they are and the state of the bodies? They're likin' the cartel for this one."

Which is exactly where we were pointing them. But his words make my stomach clench. "I'm almost afraid to ask." We gave the cleaner guidance but let him use his artistic flair.

"Let's just say someone will be playing a game of mix and match with a lot of body parts."

"Jesus." Now I do cringe. Merrick wasn't kidding about his cleaner being good at what he does. "How long before their names hit the media?"

"It's only a matter of time."

"Right." Reporters are already circling. They've sniffed out a big story. "All right. Let me know if—"

"Cameras picked up something around the airport, from the night of the explosion."

"Oh, yeah?" With all this Perri shit, I'd almost forgotten about the plane. "They catch Uncle Pete's guy there?"

"No. Not *his* guy."

I frown. Something about the way he said that sounds off. "Whose guy, then?"

"Surveillance shows Bane driving away minutes after the bomb exploded."

"*Bane*?" My father's hit man? "You sure?"

"As if I'd ever mistake that fucking face. He's like the grim reaper without the scar. With it, he makes my balls shrink."

My frown grows deeper. "But that doesn't make sense." Bane only works for one man.

My father.

"Don't know what to tell you, other than Bane was there at the time of the explosion. You should probably ask the old man about that."

"Yeah. Thanks." I end the call, an uneasy feeling settling over me.

TWENTY-ONE
MERCY

HEY, beautiful. Hotel stuff to do. Be back in a few hours. Moe's around. Order room service and stay in the penthouse.

I smile at Gabriel's scrawl on the notepad he left on his pillow, even as a twinge of disappointment stirs, that I won't be treated to a round of slow and sensual morning sex.

And, to think, there was a time when I snuck out of the bedroom to avoid him.

I laugh at myself as I stretch my sore limbs.

Climbing out of bed, I trudge to the bathroom to relieve myself. Memories of last night have me blushing as I stand naked in front of the full-length mirror. There is something about Gabriel's lack of inhibitions that is decidedly attractive.

One thing is for sure: a boring sex life is not in the cards for us.

Neither is a normal life, I remind myself somberly, as a flash of three dead bodies hits me. I struggle to push that thought aside, and it leaves me with this lingering sense of dread.

This sense that something bad is just around the corner, waiting for us.

What will it be though?

Another attack by this uncle?

Agent Lewis, making good on her promise to arrest Gabriel?

At least my father is safe for the time being.

I want Gabriel to come back. When he's with me, this doesn't feel like too much to handle.

Maybe I should take a picture of myself like this and send it to him, entice him to drop his "hotel stuff" and come back to me. At least then I wouldn't have to deal with Michelle or Moe—two awkward conversations I'd rather avoid at all costs.

With a heavy sigh, I slip on a terrycloth robe and open the door.

A man with a long, jagged scar marring the side of his face stands on the other side.

His gloved hand smothers my scream for Moe before it can escape.

I feel a sharp prick in the side of my neck as I fight against his vicelike grip.

And then my mind succumbs to darkness.

Did you enjoy Dirty Empire?
If so, please consider leaving a review!

The thrilling end to Mercy and Gabriel's sordid tale is available. Read Fallen Empire now!

SNEAK PEEK – TEMPT ME, THE WOLF HOTEL, #1

February

"I didn't mean for it to happen, Abigail. I swear!"

"You didn't mean for it to happen! You didn't mean to put your..." My words fall apart with my sobs. I can barely see Jed's face through my tears. Tears that haven't stopped since I ran for my dorm room earlier today. Tears that have left my skin raw and tight. And every time I think I'm all cried out, the image of Jed and *her* flashes inside my head and a fresh wave hits.

I wipe my dripping nose against my sweatshirt sleeve. I'm far past the point of caring what I look like. "Who is she, anyway?"

"Nobody important." He brushes his own tears away with his palm and then reaches for my face, cupping my cheeks. "You are my whole life. You've *always* been my whole life. Always! You know that, right? Tell me you know that!"

I swallow against the sharp knot lodged in my throat but

it doesn't budge. I *knew* that. Up until today. "Then why would you break my heart?"

His handsome face flinches as if I'd slapped him. Something I wish I had the nerve to do. "You weren't supposed to find out."

Oh my God! "That makes it better?"

"No, that's not what I'm saying." He hangs his head for a moment. "Look, we're getting married next year and then it's just you and me. It's been just you and me for *all* these years. And," he swallows, hesitates, "this is something I've been thinking about. A lot, lately."

"About cheating on me?"

"No! About, you know..." He winces. "Sex."

That's what this is all about? "Why didn't you tell me? I would have—"

"No, Abigail." Jed's face is suddenly stern. "You and me, we're doin' it the right way by waiting until we're man and wife. You're so innocent. So pure." He leans forward, pressing his forehead against mine. "It means everything to me that you'll give that to me on our wedding night. But"—a sheepish look overtakes his face—"I'm a guy. It's different for me."

"How is it different?" Who is this person sitting in front of me?

"Because we're weak! This is something I need to do. I need to get this out of my system, or I'm afraid I'll make a mistake down the road, when it *really* matters. Trust me on this one. You don't want me straying later on, when we have kids, do you?"

I'm listening, but I'm not believing these words coming out of Jed's mouth. "So we're breaking up?"

"No." He frowns. "Not exactly. We're taking a little breather, okay? Just until I can get my head on straight. But we're meant to be, you and me." He brushes strands of hair off my face, like he's done a thousand times. "I'll come back to you. I promise."

I'm so angry and hurt, I can't even face him anymore, so I fix my eyes on the small gumball machine promise ring he gave me on my sixteenth birthday, my sobs drowning out the rest of his words.

April

"Look directly into the camera when you answer the questions," the woman commands, her cold blue irises piercing behind a pair of trendy horn-rimmed glasses. Between those, her honey-blonde bun, the fitted black business suit and four-inch heels, she could pass for one of those librarian/strippers instead of a corporate recruiter.

I adjust my practical gold-wire-framed round spectacles. "Okay."

She readies the iPhone sitting in the stand for taping while I fidget on my stool, tucking wayward strands of my ginger hair behind my ear and smoothing the wrinkles from my shirt. I didn't come dressed for a videotaped interview. I figured this job fair would be like any other; I'd wander by some basic booths, collect a few pamphlets, and talk to representatives who want to be anywhere but a Chicago library on a Saturday.

For the most part, that's what it is. But the booth for Wolf Hotels is different. It's three times the size of the others, with sharply-dressed recruiters and an on-site interviewing station behind a screen, to help speed up the hiring process for those who meet the basic criteria.

And the only reason I made the basic criteria is because

I lied on the paper application that I filled out twenty minutes ago. Now I'm petrified of getting caught.

"Full name, please."

I've always hated being on camera. I clear my throat nervously. "Abigail Mitchell. But I go by Abbi," I'm quick to add. My mama calls me Abigail, and everyone else from my hometown calls me Abigail because of my mama. I've never liked it.

The interviewer is stone-faced. She doesn't care what I go by. "The role that you're applying for?"

"Outdoor Maintenance and Landscaping?" I think that was the official title on the application form.

"And please describe your experience that will be invaluable to us, Abigail."

"It's Abbi." I force my biggest smile and hope my annoyance doesn't show on video when they play it back later. "Sure. Well, first off, I love the outdoors. I grew up on a farm and have spent years baling hay, throwing bags of grain, and hauling buckets of water for the animals. So don't worry, I'm plenty strong." People don't believe that I am. My slim five-foot-five stature is deceiving, but one look at my body in shorts and a tank will attest that I'm feminine but honed with muscle from long days on the Mitchell farm.

I've already provided all of this information on the handwritten application form, but I guess they want the live version as well. "I've run my own landscaping company for five years, operating out of Greenbank, Pennsylvania, maintaining commercial properties with excellence." I've been pulling dandelions and cutting grass around my podunk town every summer since I was fourteen. To call what I do "landscaping" is a farce. But if it gets me this job, far the hell away from my life, I'll say anything.

"Were any of these properties hotels?"

"Yes." Never say "no" in an interview. Always find a way to spin it into a yes.

"Please tell me about these hotels."

Crap. And there it is. I've never been a good liar. "It was just one, actually. It's called the Inn. It's...an upscale bed-and-breakfast." Three rooms in an old Victorian house, run by Perry and Wendy Rhodes. I hear one of the rooms is decorated with a cat theme. Cat wallpaper, cat pillows. Cats, everywhere.

By the way the woman's painted red lips are pressed together, I'm pretty sure my answer is not the one she was looking for. "Okay. Thank you. I also see here that you worked weekends serving customers at a place called the Pearl for several years."

"Yes. That's my aunt's restaurant. I'd help her out during the busy season." I hesitated about using Aunt May as a reference. I can't be sure she'll give me a glowing recommendation if it means I won't be coming back to Greenbank for the summer. Mama would have her skin if she ever found out she helped make that happen.

"What type of establishment is it?"

"A family restaurant."

"So, not fine dining?"

I sigh. "No. I wouldn't call it that." Slapping together hot turkey sandwiches and pouring Cokes from a fountain does not make for fine dining.

"And have you ever cleaned houses professionally... No," she says, seeing me shake my head fervently, my face twisting with disdain at even the suggestion. That means dealing with fitted sheets all day long, and that sounds like torture to me.

"I see you've also done receptionist work."

Finally, something I can answer truthfully and positively. "Yes. I've worked part-time in my church's office for years. I still do, when I go home for the summer."

"What exactly did you do for them?"

"Answer phones and schedule appointments for the Reverend. I also balance the church's books and organize the annual Corn Roast weekend charity BBQ for our parish." Something I can't bring myself to do again this summer, but will be guilted into doing by my mama and the reverend, should I go back to Greenbank.

She scans my application. "I see you're in school right now." She pauses, and I realize that I'm supposed to answer her.

"Yes. I have one more year in a Bachelor of Arts degree." The right side of my face is burning from the heat of the lamp. I imagine this is what an interrogation feels like. How much longer is this going to take?

"Are you able to commit to the four-month contract, from May through August?"

"North Gate College starts in September and exams finish at the end of this month, so that won't be a problem."

She smiles. "Good. And what are your plans for after college, Abbi?"

My face falls before I'm able to control my expression. That question catches me off guard. She's talking about next summer, and all I can focus on is getting through today, tomorrow, and this summer. Ideally in Alaska.

Is this where I'm supposed to lie and say that I aspire for a career with Wolf Hotels? I debate my answer for a few heartbeats, and finally decide on the truth. "Honestly, I'm not sure anymore. I was supposed to get married and help run the family farm, but my fiancé and I are—" I stop myself with a deep breath and then an embarrassed little smile. So inappropriate for an interview. "My personal situation is in limbo," I say instead, my voice growing husky, my eyes burning with the threat of tears. It's all still too fresh, too raw. "I'll probably go back home. My family's there."

"And help run the farm?" Her eyes graze over me—over my thick braid that I can't help but toy with when I'm nervous, over my favorite royal-blue button-down that's probably been washed one too many times, over my generic jeans, and down to my Converse—and I know she's judging me. I sit up straighter, feeling more self-conscious than I already do being in front of a camera.

I look nothing like her, or any of the other recruiters here. They're all put together, with smooth, richly colored hair and perfectly painted faces. I don't wear much makeup; just a little lip gloss and, on occasion, shimmery pink nail polish. I don't use hairspray and not a drop of dye has ever touched my hair for fear that it'll make the color worse than it already is.

"Yes." That has always been the plan. But now I feel like I need to defend myself. I'm not just another farm girl, getting ready to bake pies and pop out little farm babies. "I started a side business making soaps, moisturizers, and essential oils a few years back. It's called Sage Oils. I'm going to focus on expanding that." Sage, after my favorite herb, though my products involve everything from mint to lavender to lemon. Up until this point, the bulk of my sales have been thanks to the annual Christmas bazaar and summer fair. I can't complain though; that money will pay for my flight to Homer, should Wolf hire me.

"My, you're quite the enterprising young woman. And so busy. Landscaping and soapmaking businesses, college, farming..." I can't read the woman's tone to tell if she's genuinely impressed. "And what do you do for enjoyment, Abbi?"

I bite my bottom lip to stop myself from saying "Umm" while I think. Wolf Hotels is one of the most posh lines of hotels in the world. I need to sound smart if I have a hope in hell of getting this job. "As you have noted, I'm quite busy with work and school. When I have free time, I spend it with my family, and with my church, solidifying my faith." Which is in some dicey water as of late. "I also volunteer at the local animal shelter, both here in Chicago as well as at home."

"So you like animals?"

"Yes!" I nod emphatically. "I'm excited to see Alaska's wilderness."

She offers me a tight smile. "Right. Last question. Why should we hire you to work at Wolf Cove in Alaska?"

I look down at the pamphlet in my hand—pictures of white-capped mountains and vast wilderness, glacier valleys and volcanoes.

Thousands of miles of serenity, of nothingness.

Thousands of miles from my current life.

They don't want to listen to my sob story, and it's sure as hell not going to get me hired. I struggle to smile as I stare into the camera, silently pleading with my eyes to whoever is making the hiring decisions. "Because I'm smart, hard-working, diligent, and ethical. I respect people and I love a challenge. Plus, I've always wanted to visit Alaska, and this looks like an incredible once-in-a-lifetime opportunity." I clear my throat. "I have nothing to distract my focus. I will give Wolf Cove *everything* I have to offer this summer."

She presses a button and steps around. "Great. Thank you. We'll be in touch."

"When will you be making your decisions?" It's the beginning of April; I'd be flying out in four weeks if I get hired.

"Shortly. We've already filled many of the positions from our pool of current Wolf employees who are interested in the Alaska location. We're just plugging some last-minute holes with outside recruitment." She sticks my application into a red file folder. Is that the reject file?

"Do I have a chance? Honestly." I can't believe I asked that, but I have nothing left to lose.

"We tend to hire people who already have luxury hotel chain experience. But we'll be in touch." She stands there with her arm leading the way to the exit.

My shoulders sag. I force myself to leave before I beg her to put in a good word for me.

There's no way I'm getting this job.

May

I inhale deeply, reveling in the crisp ocean air as land approaches ahead. Chicago was in the seventies when I left this morning. Two layovers, a flight delay, and fifteen hours later, the fifty-five degree day's high has dipped to low forties and I had to dig my winter jacket out of my suitcase.

"Have you ever been to Alaska before?" the captain, a soft-spoken white-haired man named John asks, his hands resting easily on the ferry's wheel.

I shake my head, my gaze drifting over the sea of evergreen and rock as far as the eye can see. We left the dock in Homer thirty minutes ago. It didn't seem like it would take that long to cross, but Kachemak Bay is vast and wide and unlike anything I've ever seen.

And on the other side of it is my home for the next four months.

I'm so glad I remembered to pop an Antivert an hour

before boarding. I'd be puking over the rails by now had I not. Boats and I have never coexisted well.

"So, what made you come?" I can tell John likes to talk, as much for conversation as to assess the foreigners coming to his homeland.

"A brochure," I answer simply, honestly.

He chuckles. "Yeah, it'll do that, all right. Lures plenty of folk our way."

I smile, though his words resonate deep inside. It "lured" me. Yes, that's exactly what it did.

Frankly, the brochure didn't need to work too hard.

When things take an ugly turn, people are always saying they're going to pick up and move far away. Australia, France, anywhere that puts an ocean between them and their problems. Most don't ever act on that. I certainly had no intention of doing so.

And then I went to that job fair in the city library, more than a little panicked about what I was going to do this summer. Recruiters were peddling administrative and counselor positions, trade internships, day care. Nothing I was interested in. Plus, they were all local Chicago-based positions. The last thing I wanted to do was stay in Chicago for the summer. I needed to separate myself from it and its bitter memories, if for only a few months until school started again in the fall.

But the idea of going back to Pennsylvania, where everyone including the cows had heard the nitty-gritty details about my breakup with Jed, was even more unappealing.

That's what happens when you grow up in a small town and then go away to college with your high school sweetheart, who's also the reverend's son, who you were supposed to marry the summer after you both graduate college.

Who you've been saving yourself for.

Who you caught with his pants down and thrusting into some raven-haired jezebel.

And, while in the depths of despair, though you know better, you tell your upstanding, churchgoing mama, who is known around town as much for her raspberry pie as for her big mouth.

That scandal sure gave the folks of Greenbank something to talk about during Pennsylvania's long, cold winter. It's been months since D-Day, or what I like to call Dick Day, when I caught him. February 2, to be exact.

I'm sure tongues were wagging across pews during church service. When I visited over Easter weekend though, I got nothing but sympathetic nods and pats. Jed, sitting in the pew directly across from us, earned more than a few glowers. Not everyone shared those feelings, though. His father, Reverend Enderbey, decided that giving a sermon on man's weakness for carnal flesh and the need for forgiveness and understanding would be more appropriate than discussing the resurrection of Christ that day.

Much like Jed promised me, Reverend Enderbey has promised my parents that this is just a momentary blip in Jed's faith; that he's feeling confused and needs to sort out his priorities. He'll come back to me, after he's done sowing his wild oats.

Why do they all think I'll want to take him back?

He broke my heart that day, and has continued breaking it daily, every time I see him walking hand in hand around campus with *her*.

He's not just sowing wild oats. They're *dating* now.

So when I passed by the Wolf Hotels booth at the job fair a month ago and spotted the pamphlet with a beautiful vista of snow-capped mountains and forest, I immediately stopped and started asking questions, and within ten minutes I knew that Wolf Cove was my ticket away from sadness, temporarily at least. I just needed to get myself to Homer, Alaska. They'd provide transportation to the hotel, subsidized accommodations and meals onsite, and weekly transport to Homer, if needed, and in turn I'd work like a dog and keep my mind occupied.

The best part? It was almost 3,800 miles from everything I know.

It sounded perfect. And unattainable. I walked out of that interview feeling hopeless, assuming that there was no way I'd get the job.

And yet I'm standing here today. I call that divine intervention. God knew I needed this miracle.

It came in the form of a phone call a week after the interview, with an official offer for a position in the Landscaping and Maintenance crew. I screamed. I even shed a few happy tears, which was a nice change from all the sad tears I've spilled since February. Knowing that I could avoid Greenbank, Jed, and my family, that I would be leaving my dorm room the day after my last exam and hopping onto a plane… that's the only reason I've held it together this long.

The ferry turns left to run along the coastline, farther into the bay.

"What are those places, over there? Do people live out here?" I point toward the little huts speckling the shore, camouflaged within the trees.

"Nah. They're mostly lodges and cabin rentals."

I study the structures, like yurts on stilts overlooking the water. "They're nice. Rustic."

"They are, indeed."

"Not like Wolf Cove, though."

John chuckles softly, shaking his head. "Not quite."

If the pictures in the pamphlet are at all accurate. My mama's convinced that it's all computer generated, that nothing that luxurious would exist up in Alaska. That I'll end up contracting West Nile from the thick fog of mosquitoes, or I'll wake up in the rickety shack that I'm sleeping in to find a bear gnawing on my leg.

To say Bernadette Mitchell is unhappy about this Alaska job is an understatement. At first she flat-out told me that I wasn't allowed to go. I hung up the phone on her that night, the first time I'd ever done that. Probably the first time *anyone's* ever had the nerve to hang up on a woman like her. I half expected her to drive the nine hours and slap me upside the head.

Two days later, after she'd cooled off, she called and tried to persuade me. I was making a grave mistake, leaving Greenbank and Jed. We'd be away from the chaos of Chicago and the temptations that made Jed stray. We'd have each other, day in and day out, and I could remind him of why we're so perfect together.

I know it's not going to be that simple.

So I dug my heels in. I've been "good girl Abbi" all my life, sitting next to my parents at church service every Sunday, keeping company with like-minded people, staying away from the "bad kids" who drank and smoked pot and had sex. Always listening to Mama.

Maybe if I'd just spread my legs for Jed, my heart wouldn't have been smashed into a thousand pieces.

While she's my mama and I know she wants what's best for me, she, too, thinks that Jed and I belong together, and that our reunion is inevitable, once he gets "the devil" out of his system. I had to bite my tongue before I pointed out to her that the girl currently sucking Jed's dick is a significant obstacle in this imminent reconciliation of ours.

I scan the approaching buildings, my excitement triumphing over my exhaustion. "Where is it?"

"Wolf Cove is just around the bend."

Wolf Cove Hotel in Wolf Cove, Alaska. "How do you go about renaming a cove, anyway?"

John chuckles softly again. He's such a pleasant man. "The cove has been Wolf Cove for hundreds of years now. The Wolf family has a lot of history up here, with the gold mines. That's where they made their first fortune. Though I'm sure they could afford to have it renamed, if it came to that. They're a successful lot. Generous, too."

Man, to be a part of that family. They must have a lot of money, to risk opening a location like this all the way up here, and set their employees up the way they're doing for us, and all the benefits. "Hey, thanks for coming back for me. I didn't want to stay in a motel." It's just John and me on the ferry, and a deck full of crates and supplies. He was kind enough to make another trip across the bay and pick me up after my flight delay. Apparently he carted a full load of college-aged employees over hours ago.

"We didn't want to leave you stranded. 'Specially on the first day. I woulda had to come back for the supplies first thing in the morning, anyway."

I glance at my watch with dismay. "I've missed the orientation session." It started at seven, almost an hour ago. The skies are deceptively light for this time of evening. "I can't believe how bright it still is."

"Wait 'til June."

"Less than five hours of darkness on the equinox, right?"

He grins. "Someone's been doin' her homework."

"I like to be prepared." The day I applied for the job, I ran home and researched Alaska late into the night instead of studying for my exams. The further I dug, the more excited I became, and the harder I prayed that I'd get the job.

"Well, I'm sure one of the ladies will be kind enough to fill you in on what you missed. They seemed like a nice group. Polite youngsters like yourself, for the most part anyway."

At twenty-one, it feels strange to be referred to as a "youngster," but I guess next to John, who's got to be pushing seventy, that's exactly what I am.

The ferry rounds the crop of small islands and turns toward the cove. John points to the massive building ahead. "And there's Wolf Cove Hotel."

My eyes widen. "Whoa. The brochure pictures weren't fake." And they don't do this place justice.

John chuckles again. "No, they certainly weren't."

I stare at it quietly, mesmerized. The main lodge towers over the water. Even from this distance, I can see that the lodge is grandiose in its design and massive in size. I can't make out the details to appreciate it yet, but there's no doubt it's something to be admired.

"They just made the finishing touches two weeks ago. Been working on it for almost three years, now."

"Is it still opening on Sunday?" Belinda, the woman who called to formally hire me, said that these first few days would be focused on training and last-minute preparations.

"I'll be ferrying in the first guests at noon. I've been bringin' employees in by the boatload over the last two days. There are a lot of you. A high staff-to-guest ratio, I heard someone say."

"How is the Wolf family going to make any money?"

"I'm guessing the twelve-hundred-dollar-a-night price tag will help."

My mouth drops open. "Who can afford that?" I barely

scraped together the eleven hundred I needed for my plane ticket here.

"What's that famous line from that movie? Oh, shucks. You may be too young to remember. The one with the baseball and all those cornfields. 'If you build it…'"

I smile. It's only my dad's favorite movie.

He winks.

We fall into a comfortable silence as we approach, and I realize that I've been rolling my promise ring around my finger unconsciously this entire time. It's been three months since Jed and I broke up and I haven't been able to bring myself to remove it. Now, I slip it off, letting the cheap metal rest in the palm of my hand. A part of me—the hurt, angry part—wants to toss it into the water and be done with it. A symbol of my faith in Jed.

But I can't bring myself to do it just yet. So, I slip the ring into my pocket and try to focus on the months to come.

Have you met Henry Wolf yet?

ALSO BY K.A. TUCKER

The Wolf Hotel Series:

Tempt Me (#1)

Break Me (#2)

Teach Me (#3)

Surrender To Me (#4)

Empire Nightclub Series:

Sweet Mercy (#1)

Gabriel Fallen (#2)

Dirty Empire (#3)

Fallen Empire (#4)

For Contemporary Romance, Women's Fiction, and Romantic Suspense by K.A. Tucker, visit katuckerbooks.com

ABOUT THE AUTHOR

K.A. Tucker writes captivating stories with an edge.

She is the internationally bestselling author of the Ten Tiny Breaths and Burying Water series, He Will Be My Ruin, Until It Fades, Keep Her Safe, The Simple Wild, Be the Girl, and Say You Still Love Me. Her books have been featured in national publications including USA Today, Globe & Mail, Suspense Magazine, Publisher's Weekly, Oprah Mag, and First for Women.

K.A. Tucker currently resides in a quaint town outside of Toronto.

Learn more about K.A. Tucker and her books at katuckerbooks.com

Printed in Dunstable, United Kingdom

74082999R00136